American Dreams

Michael Hope

Literary Fiction Ltd

https://literaryfiction.blog

literaryfiction.ltd@gmail.com

ISBN-13: 978-1-9998289-0-5
ISBN-10:1999828909

to

Good Dream dreamers

'The cause of America is in great measure the cause of all mankind. Many circumstances hath, and will arise, which are not local, but universal, and through which the principles of all Lovers of Mankind are affected, and in the Event of which, their Affections are interested.'

Thomas Paine, Common Sense, 1776

All the digital links in this book are real

Contents

Preface

It was a September morning in '75. I had only recently moved to London and it being Saturday and warm and sunny I had gone out to explore Regents Park. I was meandering in one of its gardens when at the end of a long bed of red dahlias I turned and there facing me were two people standing behind artist easels, a largish dog, head up, lying between them.

It had been a month since I, a dog lover, had engaged with a dog, so nearing this one I made eye contact, stopped and crouched down to show that I was friendly. The dog stood up and wagged its tail. Mutual cordiality now established, I walked up to the dog, saw that it was a male, presented my hand to his nose and then stroked his head and neck. He had a medium length black coat but with an orange facemask and a dense white undercoat. I had forgotten about the artists when a man's voice with an American accent said, "His name is George."

I stood up and made eye contact with the artists, first with the man who had spoken and who looked to be in his early thirties, and then with the other, a girl, not more than twelve or thirteen.

"What breed is he?" I asked.

"We don't know for sure," said the man, "because he was feral when he came to live with us. But I think he's half Siberian husky and half German shepherd."

"Where was that?"

"Back in the States in rural Wisconsin."

I came around to the artists' side of their easels and stopped in front of the man's.

"His name is Michael," said the girl, humour showing in her eyes.

"And that's my daughter Julie."

I can't remember if at this point I told them my name or not because by now I had glanced at both their paintings and I was spellbound by their juxtaposition. Both were nearly finished and both of the same view of the flower garden and yet they were profoundly different from each other. The girl's painting was in a late impressionist style and, I thought, extremely well done. Her father's was totally abstract. If in a gallery you saw his painting you would never think it was a painting of a garden and yet its palette and arrangement and balance of colours and mass were almost identical to those of his daughter's.

****

That September morning in the park so long ago was the beginning of a friendship. Michael and I took an

2

immediate liking to each other, perhaps because we were so different but both so fond of dogs. Today, forty-two years later, seven of Michael's paintings adorn the walls of my modest London flat, none of which I could ever have afforded to buy, even before Michael's paintings (and Julie's too) became celebrated. One of my seven is the abstract Michael was finishing that morning we met and which for me soon came to symbolize what I think of as the hidden half of Michael Hope's identity. As our friendship developed he made it clear that there was a segment of his life – roughly from the age of twenty-two to twenty-six when he came to the UK – that was not in any way open for discussion. Clearly he was a man who had been gravely wounded. The most he ever said to me about it was, "It was the most beautiful time of my life and now too painful to remember."

Through the decades I have honoured Michael's wish. But many an evening I have sat on my sitting room couch gazing at the painting of that beautiful garden on that beautiful morning wondering what was the beautiful but tragic story behind Michael's life.

It has been a year now since I've seen Michael. It was at the opening of his exhibition at a Mayfair gallery. As always he asked what I was up to and I told him that I was involved in setting up a website to promote and maybe publish contemporary Commonwealth literary fiction.

"What's your website's address?"

"https://literaryfiction.blog/"

3

I was surprised when Michael pulled out pen and paper and wrote it down. Early this morning I received an email from him. After a few irrelevant remarks, he writes:

> *Now as I near the end of my life and history threatens a return to darkness, I have finally screwed up my courage to write down that story that all these decades I've kept from you and from everyone else. It's attached. If you want, you're welcome to publish it (I don't care about the money) off your Literary Fiction website.*
>
> *Of course I realize it's American, not British or Commonwealth, and doesn't qualify as literary nor even as fiction. But perhaps you could label it as a new kind of fiction: fictionalized fiction. In any case I hope you will read it and forgive me for being so long in the telling.*
>
> *Almost as ever,*
> *Michael*
>
> *PS: The Julies and George V send their greetings.*

It has now gone midnight. Five hours ago I finished Michael's *American Dreams*. I am still in an emotionally and intellectually agitated state. Twenty minutes ago I published *American Dreams* and you may download it as an eBook or order it as a paperback from any Amazon.

Prologue

The summer I graduated from college my father, limited as he was, gave me two nuggets of wisdom that have been knocking about in my mind ever since. "The higher up you go," he told me, "the higher the percentage of scoundrels. And it's when those bastards start to dominate at the top that society is in big trouble."

These days my father's rough-edged maxims wouldn't win many friends in the White House or in Wall Street boardrooms, but taken together they offer, when you pause to reflect, a remarkably generous and optimistic view of humankind. Today, weighted down with maturity and beyond, I realize my father dispensed his insight on the eve of my departure for graduate school as a warning of what I might – it being America – become. But back then on the empty prairie, youthful innocence so swamped my sensibilities that I saw only how the precept tilted the moral odds in my favor.

You must not, however, let me mislead you. My foregoing appeal to my perceived disadvantagement may be only a way of excusing myself for my failure to prevent the culminating event of fifty years ago, or, for that matter, for waiting till now to commit an account of those happenings to the public record. The bitter truth is that I too, in some measure which I will leave you to judge, was nonchalantly – a free-rider if you like – carried along by the tidal wave of dreams engulfing the plains and valleys of our land. And that season when the wave broke, spilling its jetsam across my domain, I recovered out of the fetid ruins what dreams I could and retreated forever – I thought – from the public business of humanity and the maintenance of the republic.

Part One: Farewell

My mother's family crossed from England to Massachusetts before our revolution. Her grandparents, Mary and John King, were among the first pioneers to settle west of the Missouri River. In 1860 they crossed by covered wagon with their baby Coryden from Illinois to what is now the south-eastern corner of Nebraska. With the Civil War about to begin, it would be another four years before the Nebraska Territories was officially opened for settlement.

With a spade, John and Marry dug in the prairie a hole three and a half feet deep and fifteen feet square. With the sod and the earth they turned up, they built three-foot high walls around their hole, and from the banks of a nearby stream they axed down willows to support a sod roof. The following year in their new home Mary gave birth to Ellen. She died the following winter. Then in '63 Levir was born, followed by Emma in '66. In the winter of '69 an epidemic, probably cholera, hit and all three of Mary and John's surviving children died. So after ten years of homesteading there were only two Kings.

Despite the death of their four children, Mary and John managed to build a house above ground. They also continued to dream and continued to make love. Between 1871 and 1881 Mary gave birth to six more children: Helen, Mattie, Myrtle, Royal, Donna and Worthy. Mattie died in childhood, but all the others reached their seventies, and Worthy and Myrtle remained vigorous into their nineties.

My father's family came to America much later. My paternal grandfather and his two older brothers emigrated from England in 1887, disembarked in New York and within hours boarded a train headed west. They got off at Omaha. Guided by different dreams, they said goodbye, never to see each other again.

The eldest became a cowboy and eventually a small-time bachelor cattle rancher in Montana. The middle brother became a prospector, spent his life following gold and silver rushes, and mailed his last letter from Alaska in 1917. My father's father took up farming in central Nebraska. After two years he gave it up and moved to Central City where he worked in a hardware and feed store. About the time my father and his sister entered their teens, the family moved to Lincoln where the schools were better. I grew up there on Puritan Avenue.[1]

The story I am about to tell suffers from two apparent implausibilities, first that there was an "assassination" that

---

[1] You can Google-street-view Puritan Avenue here:
https://www.google.co.uk/maps/@40.7871381,-96.6767394,3a,75y,274.33h,90t/data=!3m4!1e1!3m2!1sttHGk91_0mXyw_mb26CuRw!2e0

history doesn't know about and second that the likes of me could ever become involved with the likes of the first of the four Julies. True, as a child I showed a tendency to what some would call deviance, but on the eve of my sixteenth my impeccably respectable lawyer father entombed it. He spent most summer evenings, when he was not drowsing over the *Lincoln Evening Journal*, on all-fours on his lawn looking for weeds, and on one such evening as I was leaving to meet my girlfriend, he called me over.

"In a few days, Son, you'll be sixteen. I've a proposition for you. If you promise to give up your drawing and painting and, as we have discussed, put your time and effort instead into your mathematics and other serious studies, then for your birthday I'll buy you a nice used car."

The following week I took possession of a 56 Chevy.

That was the first of three major life-turns – one for worse, one for neutral and one for better – that, with the help of others, I willed early in my life. This book is mostly about the third. My second turn began four years after the first or 84 days after King's "I Have a Dream" speech, two days before JFK's assassination and 15 months before the same of Malcom X, when my college adviser Professor Malonzo, who also lived on Puritan Avenue, called me into his office. Wearing a three-piece shrimp-colored suit and smoking Old Golds in a long ivory holder, Professor Malonzo was not your typical Lincolnite. He had that day's *Lincoln Star* spread out on his roll-top desk.

"Look at this", he said. "They print this map every so often when someone gets out of line."

The map was titled "Lincoln Residential Zones". One small thatched rectangle was labeled "Negro", an even smaller one "Indian and Mexican", and here and there across the rest of the map appeared the word "White".

"You've heard of Russell's Paradox, Mike. Well this is Malonzo's Paradox. I was born in Mexico. Both my parents were born in Mexico. I lived in Mexico until I went to Yale to do my PhD, and I'm still a Mexican citizen. But I've lived without problems on Puritan Avenue for twenty-two years."

I didn't know what to say.

"The paradox's solution requires the number four and a three syllable word. But that's not what I called you in for, Mike. I thought maybe we should have a chat about your future."

The chat turned out to be more a monologue and a rather long-winded one. The professor began by identifying three categories of people who succeed at doing higher mathematics: math geniuses who are extremely rare, "naturals" for whom learning higher math comes easy but who are not profoundly creative, and the other 95 per cent who have the capacity to learn it, but have to work very hard. He said I, like him, was a natural. I liked his term "natural" because rather than taking pride in my math talent I'd always regarded it as just something I'd been born with.

"Am I correct in presuming, Mike, that maybe you're thinking of becoming a mathematics professor like me?"

"Yes."

"Well that's a realistic ambition, and I'm sure you'd be better at it than me. But I've thought of another possible future for you, also academic, that you probably haven't thought of and that might have advantages for you that the strictly mathematics one doesn't."

First, he mapped out the road for me if I went for the math professor option. It wasn't quite what I had imagined. He said that with my grades I could go to whatever university I fancied to do a PhD. But if I went, say, to Harvard or Berkeley, I would no longer find myself at the top of the heap because some of my fellow students would be mathematical geniuses. Worse, when I finished, the doors of top rank universities would probably not be open to me for a career, because not only was I not a math genius, I also would not have an undergraduate degree from a prestigious university.

Then came the alternative: I could become an economist.

"Economics has an infatuation with mathematics. And it seems to be intensifying. But in that profession math naturals are extremely rare and math geniuses unknown. So if you were to go for a PhD in economics it would be like going for a PhD in math if you were a math genius. And when you finished you could have a career in elite universities. You've already taken a half dozen economics courses as electives. If you were to take some more, every economics PhD program in the world will find you irresistible."

****

A year and a half later — it was now June '65 — I graduated. Berkeley had accepted me as a graduate student, and in August, before moving to Berkeley, I went travelling with two fraternity brothers to Europe. Looking back I can see that that mild adventure planted in me a subversive seed. It was not that I was abroad for the first time that was significant. One can travel the whole world without ever leaving home in one's mind. What made the difference was that for the first time I let myself go with someone whose suppositions in life were qualitatively different from mine. Her name was Vanessa. She was the daughter of two East Coast writers and about to begin her final year at Vassar. Earlier in the summer she had visited Frank Lloyd Wright's Taliesin in Wisconsin and had come away with the conviction that she had to become an architect. "Who ever heard of a woman architect?" I asked ten minutes after meeting her. "All the more reason," she replied. I thought of mentioning my childhood obsession with drawing and painting, but decided not.

It was Vanessa who suggested I ditch the companionship of my fraternity brothers in favor of hers. We'd only known each other for twenty minutes. We were in London sitting at a table in the dining room of the Holland Park youth hostel and they had just announced that in ten minutes we all had to retire for the night to our respective dormitories.

"I know it's shocking to suggest that we do this when we've only just now met, but here's the way I see it. It's going to sound a bit crazy, but I didn't think this up for myself. I got it from my Dad. It goes like this. There's bad luck and there's good luck and we all know that the possibility of very bad luck can appear very suddenly and when it does we must act immediately to avoid it, like jumping back onto the curb to avoid being run over. And so we all grow up trying to avoid very bad luck and most of us do. But good luck often works the same way only backwards. It can happen suddenly as a passing chance and if you don't grab it as it passes it's gone and usually forever. My Dad says most people miss out on most of the good luck that comes their way because we aren't taught to grab hold of it before it's gone. I spotted you last night, or you spotted me with that shy smile of yours, and now I've got to know you a little and I've got this strong feeling that if I were to go travelling with you for my last two weeks I'd enjoy it a lot more than if I go alone or with those two girls over there. And you're leaving tomorrow. So this is my first and last chance to grab hold of what could be my good luck, and who knows, maybe yours too. Anyway, I'll give you the whole night to think about it. I'll see you at breakfast."

I still had not said anything. Vanessa stood up, managed a smile and left for the women's dorm.

For two weeks we thumbed around England and Scotland, some nights staying in youth hostels and some nights sleeping together at B-and-Bs, where, when checking in, we flashed the rings we had bought at a Woolworths. Back in London we found a cheap Bloomsbury hotel for our final night together. The next day when we said goodbye forever in front of the British Museum, Vanessa handed me a small package. "Don't open it until you get to Berkeley." We had browsed in Foyles the day before, and I could feel it contained three books.

13

AMERICAN DREAMS

A week later I enrolled as an economics graduate student at the University of California at Berkeley. I chose it over Harvard because it offered me more money: my life financed for three years with no duties beyond my studies. Berkeley had been in the national news a lot the previous academic year because of something called the Free Speech Movement. This was before there was anything called The Sixties, but the Berkeley scene and what was starting to happen just across the bridge in San Francisco was its beginning. Vanessa, more up on it than me, had feared the place would freak me out.

I was worried too but for different reasons. Today I still find it hard to explain even to myself the changes my head went through between landing in that new world and meeting Julie twenty-six months later. At first I didn't take much in. The hardest thing getting used to was not having a car. My Chevy had died in July and I couldn't afford to buy a replacement and the only going-away present that my father gave me was a three-year subscription to *Time* magazine. This wasn't as silly as it sounds. Like any 22-year-old I was historically naïve. I had no idea that culturally and sociologically speaking the period in which I had grown up and which still prevailed was by American standards exceptional. The Great Depression followed by World War Two had created among the populace a hunger for a return to normalcy and the predictable. So when the war ended, inevitably conformity came to rule and then, with the passing of the decades, became the new American tradition, and the longer it prevailed the more extreme it became. From time to time voices of dissent rumbled in the distance, but none, not even King's "I Have a Dream" speech the year before, had been quite so audible on Main Street as the Berkeley Free Speech Movement.

What was it? Well traditionally, at the foot of Telegraph Avenue just outside the main gate to the campus, students had recruited funds and followers for off-campus activities such as civil rights projects and political campaigns. But that year the university banned such activity along this stretch and here is how *Time* described what happened next.

> *Thousands of students responded by staging a protest that trapped a police car summoned to arrest a defiant recruiter. While police and their prisoner, Jack Weinberg, huddled for 32 hours inside the patrol car, students and off-campus agitators battered it, rocked it, used the roof as a speaker's rostrum. Stunned, the university vacillated over its next move, then suspended eight ringleaders of the demonstration.*

The students fought back with an occupation.

> *. . . "Have love as you do this thing," cooed Folk Singer Joan Baez, "and it will succeed." . . . Marching behind their Joan of Arc . . . a thousand undergraduates of the University of California at Berkeley stormed four-story Sproul Hall, the school's administration building. For 15 hours they*

camped in the corridors, whanged guitars, played jacks, watched Charlie Chaplin movies.

Then, on orders from Governor Pat Brown, 400 policemen swept into the building. The students sprawling over the littered floors offered no defiance. They went limp, and for the next 13 hours police dragged them along hall ways, pushed them into elevators or bumped them down stairs, and shoved them into buses backed up at the rear entrance. "This is wonderful, wonderful!" shouted Protest Leader Mario Savio, 21 . . . Girls were carted off to the city jails; boys were hauled to the Santa Rita prison farm, where tough criminals in blue denims watched dumb founded as guitar-laden, bearded students were herded in.[2]

****

As I've told you, it was purely a matter of financial expediency that in The Sixties' second year I came to live in its epicenter. Day by day the century's biggest social revolution pulsated and sometimes exploded around me. I scarcely noticed. Living with non-Nebraskans, even if they were would-be economists, provided me with more than enough cultural shock. They came mostly from East Coast elite schools and from abroad, especially India, Greece and Latin America.

[2] Here is a YouTube video of "The Man in the Police Car":
http://www.youtube.com/watch?v=MufwTCgodmM
And here is a bit of what followed:
https://www.youtube.com/watch?v=safaLBJKgJc

But it was not just what for me was the novelty of the people who surrounded me that kept me from noticing what was happening just beyond their shoulders. I had been in Berkeley only a week when I discovered the perverse allure of a big research library's stacks. Beyond the long suggestive curve of Memorial Library's checkout desk was an entryway into the subterranean labyrinth of aisles running between 52 miles of shelves housing 9 million volumes. Every aisle was visually identical to the aisle you had just walked down and to the aisle you were about to walk down, a uniformity of paper, concrete and steel that had the effect of exaggerating my emerging new identity. Half of every day I housed myself down there in my own five-by-five "study carrel". Some days, feeling brave, I ventured out of my cell and above ground and up to an upper floor and found a table where I could see out a window and down on what from up there seemed an imaginary world.

I had been indulging this existence for about a month when early one evening after spending most of the day in my carrel, I stepped nervously out into the other world. The sun had already set and the campus felt deserted. But in the near distance you could hear someone speaking on a loud speaker. I figured it was happening in the huge athletic field just behind the big student cafeteria toward which I was heading. As I neared the cafeteria a roar from a crowd drowned out the speaker.

A few minutes later carrying my loaded tray, I spotted two fellow econ grad housemates, Nelson and Bill, motioning for me to join them. I've forgotten Bill's last name, but "Nelson Dunnefeller Jr." has proved

17

unforgettable. Like me, Bill and Nelson wore the official uniform: loafers, kakis, a check shirt and a navy blazer. Bill wore pennies in his loafers, and Nelson's blazer, as he frequently mentioned when he was not displaying its label, was from Brooks Brothers. As I sat down, they were in the middle of a conversation.

"It's that asshole Norman Mailer," said Bill.

"Who's he?" asked Nelson.

"A novelist," I answered.

"Oh God, one of those."

"What are you guys talking about Norman Mailer for?"

"He's the asshole on the mike out there winding up all the dumb-dumb suckers."

"What's going on?"

"Don't you know?"

"Mike, remember, is from Nebraska," said Nelson in his East Coast preppy accent.

"Well, he knows who Norman Mailer is, which is more than you, Nelson. The Vietnam Day Committee is staging a protest against the war, Mike."

Bill, except when it came to other races and the other sex and the Other in general, was more egalitarian than Nelson and, despite my grasslands peculiarities, seemed to accept me as a full member of what he called "the white male human race". Nelson may have held allegiance to a similar category but was too class-assured to say so. Nonetheless he worried me more than Bill worried me, and not because of his attachment to labels and his supercilious manner nor even the glass of milk that he insisted upon drinking with every meal, but because of his snake eyes.

"Well it's not a big deal then," I said. "I've read about their demos and they never get more than 200."

"This time it's different. I had a peek on the way here and there're thousands out there," said Bill.

"Thousands of commies. It's scary," said Nelson.

"And don't forget the asshole," I added.

"Anyway, better an asshole than a cunt," said Bill.

"You've switched the topic," said Nelson. "Now you're talking about economics."

One of our professors was stressed about a woman economist – the only one we had ever heard of – who was creating difficulties for his most cherished beliefs. Her code name in his seminars was "the Cambridge cunt".

"Yes, I have, because the cunt threat is more serious than the commie threat."

"That's debatable," said Nelson.

After the debate and after we had finished eating I walked alone over to the foot of Telegraph Avenue, a narrow non-avenue-like street that runs down from Oakland and ends unceremoniously at the main entrance to the campus. Lined with bookshops, coffee houses, eateries and boutiques, and usually buzzing with students, academics and bohemians, *Time* called it America's Left Bank. The anti-war demonstrators were about to exit the fenced athletic field and come onto Bancroft Way before turning to march down Telegraph, now lined three or four deep on both sides with people waiting to see them go by. Standing on the sidewalk just beyond the campus boundary and with a view straight down the center of Telegraph was a cluster of six men being addressed by a seventh. I moved in close to listen.

"We know it's difficult to count marchers, especially peace marchers. So we've thought of a way to make it easier. They're going to come by in groups of 100 each, consisting of ten rows of ten marchers. This way we'll all be able to count exactly how many protesters there are, and you'll know how many to report. To make it even easier for you, I'm going to count out loud the groups of 100 as they go by."

There were the placards – "Male Love, Not War", "Give Peace a Chance", "Resist the Draft", "War is Hell, Don't Go", "No Vietnamese Ever Called Me a Nigger", "Girls Say Yes to Men Who Say No" – but otherwise nothing to see except the marchers who looked surprisingly ordinary. At first catcalls – "traitors" and "commies" mostly – came from the sidewalks, but as the hundreds became thousands silence prevailed except for the footfalls of the thousands marching by.

Most of an hour must have passed.

"One hundred."

Two of the journalists had disappeared. Three were scribbling in their notebooks and another was chatting up a pretty coed.

"One hundred and forty-three." It was the last. Three reporters remained. "There," said the jubilant counter. "Over fourteen thousand people marched tonight in this protest against the Vietnam War."

The reporter standing next to me was my age and with a similar dress style and we had already exchanged a few words.

"Are you going to report that?" I asked.

"I can't."

"What do you mean you can't?"

"I'd like to. Really I would."

"Well then, why don't you?"

"Because I'd lose my job. As I was leaving this afternoon my editor called me in to his office. He said if more than 5,000 turned up for this march, I should look for another job."

The next morning I bought two newspapers. The headline in the *San Francisco Chronicle* read "5,000 March Against the War". Its rival, the *Examiner*, reported 8,000. The following week I read in *Time* that there had been 12,000.

****

As Professor Malonzo had predicted, my fellow graduate students, with a couple of exceptions, were not natural mathematicians. From the first week of classes I could see them struggling with the math. So I made myself available as a tutor, informally and free of charge of course. Word got around and by the time of that first big march I had an expanding circle of "friends". The married ones invited me around for dinner, and when sisters – all the economics graduate students were male -- came to visit big brother in famous and now notorious Berkeley, I sometimes got invited to show them the nightlife. But there wasn't any, not really, unless you count the bomb that went off one night in April just after I'd gone to bed. My room shook. Immediately I guessed the target: the Vietnam Day

Committee had their offices in a house a block and a half away. I got dressed and went out. I had guessed right. A dozen police and emergency vehicles arrived, sirens blaring, but no one had been killed or seriously injured. Twenty-five months later when I surreptitiously left Berkeley no arrests had been made.

****

It was early one evening near the end of my first California year that I began to deviate accidentally from the straight and narrow. Every May an eminent economics professor – it's best not to name him – threw a huge party in his almost-a-mansion house high up in the Berkeley Hills. Old-timers called it the Bank of America Party because of the fees they knew he charged for his frequent public support of the bank's aspirations.

When I arrived, upwards of a hundred of my fellow grad students, all male, remember, and mostly womanless and like me attired in khaki identikit, were downing highballs and devouring T-bones and in loud voices displaying their knowledge of multipliers and production functions. Mixing with them were professors, mostly in brown suits and many with spaniel-like wives attached to their arms. Even back then in my toddler-adulthood I sensed it was one of those rooms full of people whose smiles in the course of the whole long evening would never reach their eyes. Mini-skirted undergrads bearing trays of drinks slid like glow worms between the guests, unaware of the disapproving looks cast their way by the professors' wives. My hope for having a better time rose when I spotted a long line of

French doors gleaming with gold and wide open to the warm breezy evening. Heading for the nearest, I sidestepped four elderly professors, slipped behind an overpopulated sofa and stepped out onto a broad open terrace. In front of me beyond the flagstones, the party spilled out into a vast subtropical garden.

And so holding an iced pinkish concoction and remembering to stand up straight, I escaped into this lush warm green expanse. At first, stepping down onto the plush-feeling lawn and looking westward, all I could see was a big orangey-gold disk low in a strangely deep blue sky. Then there below the great glowing disk and almost touching, gleamed San Francisco, its hilly profile spiked by the Bank of America skyscraper. But my Great-Plains eyes told me all this was just a phantasy. So I turned around and looked eastward, took a deep breath and then a sip of my pink concoction, sickly-sweet, and re-landed in the party. Now with my real-world thoughts turning quickly, as they did, to the possibility of women, I scanned my fellow guests. The male/female ratio was lower than you'd expect at a Sunday social at a Franciscan monastery but not by much. I slid past a conversational group of six or seven, its lone woman balanced on its outer edge like an apricot on the rim of a bowl of onions. Out of compassion I tossed her a smile. She declined to reciprocate – out of indifference or indecision I couldn't tell – and I walked deeper into the garden and deeper still until I was beyond all the guests. Now there was just the phantasy world gleaming there in front of me. My eyes were beginning to adjust to the bewitching light and just to the right of the magical city – I was still not dead-sure it was real – I saw the Golden Gate

Bridge and then a white wall of fog fast approaching it from off the ocean.

I had been sitting on a bench oblivious of the party for an unknown number of minutes when I realized someone was standing just behind me. I turned around. It was the apricot.

"Beats the party, doesn't it," she said. She was my age and immediately appealing but, like the view across the bay, she didn't fit into any of my real-life categories.

"Yeah, I've read about it, but this is the first time I've seen it."

"The *sun*?"

When I laughed, she laughed and we exchanged real smiles.

"It looks like a giant bed with a white curtain behind it," I said.

"The bridge?"

"Yeah," and we laughed again.

"Well," she said, "then it's a gay's bed what with those high posts and the twinkly sashes suspended between them."

"'A gay's? What does that mean?"

"You're obviously from a different planet. 'Gay' means a male homosexual."

We laughed again and she sat down next to me on the bench.

"This your first time at this party?" I asked. "It's an annual thing I'm told."

"It's my first as a guest."

"As a guest? What did you come as before? No, let me guess. You came as a gate-crasher from the anthropology department."

I expected her to laugh, but she didn't.

"My foster parents have a catering business and they used to cater this party. I worked for them and still do."

I was becoming infatuated. "You want to know a secret?"

"Already?"

"My name is Mike."

I had her smiling again. "Mine is Sue."

"I've never been in a place like this before."

"Obviously."

Again we laughed.

"You dream of having a house like this?" I asked.

"God no. I dream of having my own bathroom. Have you ever lived with three young women, all on the make?"

"Not yet."

"Well you wouldn't like it. The bathroom is always occupied. So now I come home at two after my last class and have the place all to myself for a few hours. It's my heaven time."

"When you're not in Heaven, what do you study."

"I don't know if you can call it studying, but I'll graduate in social work at the end of summer school. I had a couple of years out."

"Doing what?"

"One as a quasi-student in Madrid and another in Mexico City."

"I've had 22 years quasi-out in Nebraska."

As she laughed her hand started to reach out to touch mine. Then she caught herself.

"I must go back. My boyfriend will be wondering what has happened to me. It's been nice meeting you."

Without further words she stood up, turned her back on me and strode rapidly across the lawn toward the big house with the throngs of economists jabbering on its terraces.

I was devastated. Not really of course, but sitting there on the bench I had not felt so lifted – even if for only ten minutes – since I said good bye to Vanessa. I had forgotten such possibilities in life existed. The Golden Gate Bridge had disappeared behind the fog, and white fingers of the fog were now snaking their way between the lower reaches of the city's great hills. I walked back up to the party and found Bill and Nelson Jr. and some other people I knew. I wasn't hungry. A smiling drinks tray found me and I downed a glass of red wine. I was beginning to acquire a taste for wine. I was on my third glass and a prisoner to a somnambulatory discussion of statistical regression analysis when Sue, my new acquaintance, approached with a young Indian in tow. I recognized him as a fellow econ grad student but more advanced than me. In his pale grey Nehru jacket he stood out from the crowd.

"Mike, this is my boyfriend, Avi."

I liked Avi immediately. But our meeting was only a formality. We exchanged pleasantries and then Sue and Avi said good bye and headed for the front door. Although surrounded by people, I now found myself alone again. I turned, hunched my shoulders and squeezed through a gaggle of agitated econometricians, mumbled an apology, slipped behind two abandoned wives, stepped up to a picture window and saw Sue and Avi gliding in the soft shadows across the wide velvety lawn. Sipping my wine, I watched them hand-in-hand begin the long descent, step-by-step fading into the deepening twilight until all I could see was Sue's dress, moonlit apricot, fluttering in the breeze.

I left the party alone. It was deep night now as I walked down from the wealthy hills and into the more humble Northside. The tree-domed streets were deserted and violet dark. From open windows in the family houses soft voices drifted out to the sidewalk. In front of me the white globes of street lights flickered behind the low branches of the trees. The houses had small lawns and big lighted windows, some with silhouettes moving behind golden blinds. For a few long minutes as I strolled I drifted back to Puritan Avenue, Plymouth Street, Rathbone Road, my old haunts. Coming back to the present was a jolt. There was no belonging now, neither back there nor here, and no feeling that I really knew where I was going. I had strolled off the map and into melancholy. I passed a young couple kissing in the shadows. I was relieved when I reached the campus, pitch dark, no one about that I could see and tonight evocative of nothing.

****

Although in our polite words at the end of our first meeting Sue had suggested we might meet again, we both knew the odds were against it. But late Sunday night a few weeks later as I was headed home and about to cross the dark campus I spotted Sue on the opposite side of the street walking arm-in-arm with a young man who was not Avi. I stopped, turned around, waited a moment, then followed them. A few minutes later they climbed some steps to a house and Sue stepped forward to unlock the door.

The following Tuesday afternoon at two-thirty I went to that door and, below a card which bore four women's names one of which was Susan Ruccio, I pressed a brass button.

Sue opened the door and immediately froze. Neither of us spoke. I watched the expression on her face change from amazement to quandary to curiosity.

"I got lucky," I said.

"When?"

"Late Sunday evening walking alone on Euclid Avenue."

She thought for a few seconds and her face darkened. "So now you've come to blackmail me?"

"Don't be stupid. You going to invite me in?"

"Why should I?"

"Because we're attracted to each other."

"I know."

"Well then?"

"It's more complicated than you think."

She took a step back, so I walked in. She slammed the door behind me.

"How did you mean 'attracted'?"

I hesitated. "Emotionally mainly."

"Fuck!"

The genders were different back then and it was the first time I had ever heard a woman say "fuck".

28

"Fuck what?"

"Fuck, that's what I'm afraid of."

"Why?"

"I'm not the standard package."

"How so?"

"You ever say more than two words at a time?"

Of course we laughed and harder than any time before and when she brushed against me, my arm went behind her back and our eyes locked, but when we were about to kiss she broke away. She was wearing a thin bathrobe and nothing else. I followed her through the apartment and into her small bedroom. Next to her bed we stood facing each other, but neither of us spoke and when she glanced away I could tell she was sizing up her options.

"I may be bad, Mike, but not as bad as it probably looks to you. "

"I'm open-minded."

"But maybe not as much as you think."

"Try me."

"Why should I trust you?"

"With what?"

"My secret."

"Your secret? Well, sure I could promise not to ever tell anyone. But so could anyone."

"But what about you, Mike?"

"What about me?"

"Do you promise?"

"Sure, if you want me to. But if I understand that you're telling me something in confidence I don't need to promise not to tell."

"I've never told it straight to anyone before."

"I'd never been to a party like that one where we met before."

"This is more serious, Mike. Sit down."

I sat down next to Sue on the bed.

"I picked Avi out as my steady boyfriend partly because I'm fond of him and partly because when it comes to women, at least women like me, he's naïve. You may be more naïve than Avi generally, but not, I think, as naïve when it comes to women."

"So?"

"So you would figure me out."

"Meaning what?"

"The reason I was in care, Mike – I told you, didn't I, that I have foster parents?"

"Yes."

"The reason why was that my mother was and is a prostitute."

Her brown eyes were looking up at me now, gauging my reaction. I was struggling to keep my cool.

"Where does she work?"

"San Francisco. My foster parents were wonderful to me, but they didn't have me all the time and they weren't the only emotional dimension to my childhood and adolescence. The short of it is that I can't bring myself to be sexually faithful."

She waited for my response.

"But neither do you want to hurt your man."

"That's it exactly."

After we finished making love – and it *was* love of a sort – we lay on her bed smoking filter tip cigarettes. Back then most young people smoked.

"In case you're interested," she said. "I only ever come if I'm gone down on."

I had to think for a minute what she meant.

"Ok, next time I will."

"Next time? What makes you think . . . ."

"How about every Tuesday and Thursday afternoon?"

****

And so it came to be. But with a proviso. Sue made me agree that at the end of summer school when she would be taking up a social worker position in Oakland and moving there, we would cease to see or even communicate with each other. Meanwhile twice a week for the next six I rang Sue's bell at half-two. Our lovemaking was usually preceded by sharing a joint – a new experience for me – and, not counting the joint, included our both committing, as Sue sometimes reminded me, one or more felonies and was followed by disjointed conversation against backgrounds of Beatles, Baez and Dylan and on one occasion Alice B. Toklas brownies. By half-four I was gone. At the beginning of August Sue moved out – I knew not where – and I retreated to Nebraska for a month.

****

Returning to Berkeley in September, I threw myself completely into my studies as I had the year before. In

31

October I did manage to hear Senator Robert Kennedy speak to nine thousand in the Greek Theatre and there again the following Saturday heard Stokley Carmichael speak about racism to nearly as many.   But nothing happened really worth telling you about until late Friday afternoon the thirteenth of January when my housemate Nelson Dunnefeller Jr. called me downstairs to the phone. It was Sue. She wanted me to go with her the next day to San Francisco's Golden Gate Park to attend what she called "The Human Be-In". I had no idea what she was talking about.   After I accepted I walked up to Telegraph Avenue and bought the new *Berkeley Barb* from a street vender wearing a Mexican poncho and a red fez. Be-In news covered its front page.

> *Materialism and empire have thwarted and veiled the spiritual foundations of man and woman and their relations in America. Profit and Desire are one-tenth of the divinity of man. We declare the necessity of spiritual exercise, experience and celebration for the proper education of man. We declare and prophesy the end of wars, police states, economic oppression and racism.*
>
> *When the Berkeley political activists and the love generation of the Haight Ashbury and thousands of young men and women from every state in the nation embrace at **the Gathering of the Tribes for a Human Be-In** at the Polo Field in Golden Gate Park the spiritual revolution will be manifest and proven. In unity we shall shower the country with waves of ecstasy and purification.*

> *Fear will be washed away; ignorance will be exposed to sunlight; profits and empire will lie dying on deserted beaches; violence will be submerged and transmuted in rhythm and dancing; racism will be purified by the salt of forgiveness.*
>
> *Bring food to share, bring flowers, bears, costumes, feathers, bells, cymbals and flags.*

Entertainment and enlightenment was promised in the form of the Grateful Dead, Jefferson Airplane, Quicksilver Messenger Service, Big Brother & the Holding Company, the poets Allen Ginsberg, Gary Snyder and assorted gurus.

****

I awoke the next morning to hear on the news that the *New York Times* had revealed that the US Army was conducting secret germ warfare experiments. Sue arrived at ten and I took her up to my room. Half an hour later she asked me what I was going to wear.

"The usual?"

"Mike, you can't."

"Why not?"

"Well, you can if you want, but it would be stupid. Obviously I'm not a hippy – or a freak as they call themselves – but neither am I a reactionary."

"So?"

"So and I'm not totally clueless as to what's going on on the other side of the Bay. I've been to the Haight-Ashbury a few times and to the Avalon Ballroom once."

"But why should I dress up silly?"

"Different."

Ok, why should I dress up different?"

"Because non-conformity is their way and whatever their failings they are the best hearts of our generation and you're going to *their* party and it's the biggest party you'll ever go to and if you dress like you usually do, you won't have half the fun."

"Alright then, dress me."

"You can start by putting on your underpants."

Sue's in-the-nude rummage through my wardrobe turned up nothing suitable.

"Bring your checkbook. The shops in the Haight-Ashbury will be closed today, but I know of a shop on Polk Street."

****

The Bay Bridge connecting Berkeley and Oakland to San Francisco is five miles long and ugly. But when you're rolling along on the upper deck, there in front of you are the city's great hills and towers coming closer and closer. And although it was mid-January, on this day it was warm, the sky cloudless blue, and I was happy and excited and Sue maybe even more so, and all the while the closer we got to the city the more the glass in the towers gleamed and shimmered.

An hour later, looking at myself in the headshop's full-length mirror, I saw a stranger: red and black striped bellbottoms (paid for by Sue), a purple and green paisley shirt, a faded denim jacket, a double strand of turquoise beads and a fluorescent yellow headband.

Sue maneuvered her car into a space alongside Golden Gate Park's panhandle. From the steady stream of hippies in feast-day garments walking by, you would think the event – I still had not come around to calling it The Be-In – was a mere hundred yards away. Not so. It was at the far end of the park, a two-mile hike, and as Sue locked up the car and arranged daisies in her hair, my striped bellbottoms earned compliments from the passing tribes. Disoriented, I hooked arms with Sue and we stepped into the psychedelic flow.

It is difficult to describe how something looked and felt to someone from a world that had neither seen nor imagined such a thing before. The huge tree-surrounded field of dancing color was spellbinding not only for me but also the whole world when it watched it on the evening news. The world's media was agog and apoplectic. "How dare they?" "What's it about?" "How can there be so many?" "Forty thousand". "Fifty thousand". No, those were exaggerations, but twenty thousand certainly, thirty thousand probably. Sue and I were late arrivals, the small stage faintly visible in the distance, the sound system crap. But it didn't matter; the audience was the main show and we all knew it and our numbers were still growing by the minute.

Pot smoke overpowered the incense. Fifty shades of cerise, magenta and chartreuse outshined the sun. The fully zonked did their thing. Who could fly their freak flag the highest? Acid rock melted animosities, mantras were chanted, teenage beauties danced topless. Dogs wearing neckerchiefs cavorted. Children with painted faces wandered in the nude. Long-haired moms and dads pushed baby carriages. Men with pony-tails carried picnic hampers. A white-haired woman, swaying to Grateful Dead rhythms, held a loaded roach-clip in one hand, a cane in the other. All orthodoxies were in a state of fundamental violation. I was surrounded by adult faces which had not yet become masks. Someone descended into the fairy tale from the sky on a parachute. Two enchanting creatures introduced themselves to me as Suzy Doozy and Judy Lovebody. It was my trousers I figured. My Sue had drifted off. Suzy Doozy said the acid had arrived. What do you mean? Owsley has brought thousands of hits. Who is Owsley? Stanley Owsley, the famous kitchen chemist, the Henry Ford of acid. Really? Yes, he's brought thousands of sugar cubes and turkey sandwiches to give away. Wow!

Despite my wow, I had no intention of dropping acid. Not in a million years. But when Sue did not reappear and Doozy and Lovebody drifted off after getting me stoned on their Panama Red, I found myself adopted by a small clan, the real thing apparently because they said they had a commune in the Haight. Wow! At some point a silver bucket passed our way and the lovely bra-less young woman leaning on my shoulder slipped a blue-tinted sugar cube between my lips. Wow!

****

Don't worry; I am not going to bore you with an account of my trip. My first trip and only trip ended the next morning when I awoke about ten. I did not know where I was, except that I was lying in a bed, a mattress on the floor, and my bed companion, like me, was nude. Unlike me she was sound asleep.

There was a window with blue curtains with sunshine filtering through, and close by another mattress with the shapes of two bodies under its orange and blue bedspread and next to it a straight-backed chair. I spotted my striped bellbottoms draped over the chair, thought of my wallet and sprung to my feet. I was counting my money when a girl suddenly sat upright in the bed next to the chair.

She had left her contact lenses on a book on the chair and now one lens was missing. I had sent it flying when grabbing my bellbottoms. She crawled out from under the covers and onto the floor. Like me she was slender and nude. I got down on all-fours and crawled beside her and thought of my father on his lawn looking for weeds. We crawled back and forth between the mattresses. Neither of the sleepers stirred. Then I found her lens and I felt relieved and happy. She thanked me with a smile, then placed the lens back on the book on the chair and got back under the covers and closed her eyes.

I slipped into my underwear, my bellbottoms and paisley shirt and picked up my denim jacket and my shoes and socks and crept out into a hallway. The light was dim. I passed five or six closed doors and came to a narrow stairway, probably once the servants'. I was desperate to pee. On the floor below, things were on a grander scale and I found a bathroom

I descended a wide carpeted staircase to the ground floor. No one was about. I heard some dreamy music and peered into a side parlour. A young woman all in white was playing a flute. I turned around and went outside. It was sunshine and blue-sky again and I could smell the sea. A block up to the left, streams of people were crossing the street, and I walked up to the corner and read the street sign. It was *Time* magazine's dreaded Haight Street; its broad sidewalks were busy with the people who called themselves "freaks".

I hadn't walked ten yards on Haight Street before my bellbottoms began receiving favourable attention. Their broad pleated bottoms fluttered in the wind and their red and black stripes vibrated in the sunlight. I realized I had to get out of them before returning to Berkeley on the bus. Haight Street was not what you might have expected. It had a small town feel and, despite the freaks, a quaint feel too because of the street's Victorian gingerbread architecture. But it was the world's worst street for depsychedelizing. I passed Himalayan Dreams, The Weed Shop, Beyond the Beyond, The Laughing Racoon Gallery, Mnasidika, Head Quarters and Far Fetched Foods. From out of the door of The Love Burger stretched an orderly line of flamboyantly dressed freaks. When I came to a coffeehouse called "I/Thou" I went in.

By Berkeley standards it was a small coffeehouse. With twenty people scattered about, it was half-full. I sat down with a double espresso at a small wooden table in a back corner. When the espresso machine was not steaming, you heard the clicking of saucers and the murmuring of voices. It felt good being there and I was glad for the double shot of caffeine. I was glad too for the chance to step back from the world and maybe regain my bearings. I had finished my espresso when a young black man wearing a yellow shirt and holding a broad hardback notebook like bookkeepers used to use, asked if he could read me one of his poems. "I'm Dandelion," he said.

"I'm Mike."

Dandelion sat down beside me. It was a short poem and Dandelion had a lovely deep voice. I bought a handwritten copy of his poem for fifty cents. It's one of the things I took with me when I left Berkeley. By now the paper has yellowed and is disintegrating at the folds, but the handwriting, loopy and upwards slanting, is still legible.

Particle of Star Dust

Oh particle of star dust,
So hard and wet and round,
What makes you spin
Round and round and round?

Gravity says all, says all
Makes the cream rise
And the bows bend
And the waters spread
And makes my body lie down.

But what makes me stand up
And cry out
As I spin
Round and round and round?

When I returned to the street the sun had gone behind a cloud and the queue at The Love Burger had vanished. I crossed over to the other side of the street and started walking. Several blocks down I came to The Psychedelic Shop and went in. Its blue, orange and gold display of incense would have masked the smell of a marijuana bonfire, and its selection of hash and marijuana paraphernalia was probably the world's largest. I thought of buying Sue a silver-plated roach-clip, but then remembered I had no way of contacting her. A large tent improvised out of Indian bedspreads stood at the shop's rear. The sign over its crawl-in entrance said "Meditation Room". I peeked in. Except for a couple who were balling, the girl on top, it was empty.

When I came to a shop called In Gear I went in. It sold blue jeans, stacks and stacks of them, but all of a sort I had never seen before. They were decorated with slits and patches. I found a pair with slits just above the knees that fit me and left the shop with my bellbottoms in a brown paper bag.

The trip back to Berkeley alone on the bus on the Bay Bridge's clanky lower deck was a downer. It was already afternoon when I put my key in the lock and re-entered econ grad student life. Nelson and Bill and a couple more of my housemates were lounging in the living-room. Like most of America they had by now seen footage of the Be-In on television and they were sitting there chatting about it. When they asked me what I thought of it and I told them I had been there, they refused to believe me. That pissed me off for some reason. I pulled out my striped bellbottoms and waved them in their faces. First silence, then giggles, then roars of laughter.

A few days later *Time Magazine* was more respectful:

> *Not a single fight marred the Be-In, and as the sun went down (to the sullen wail of Ginsberg blowing a*

conch shell), the forgathered hippies quietly cleared every bit of litter from the park. Officials later said that they had never seen so large a crowd leave so clean a field.

****

I never saw Sue again. I buried my Be-In clothes in my steamer trunk and climbed back onto the straight and narrow road leading to a Ph.D. True, that spring I went on my first peace march, but by then even economists were at least discussing the war and on April ninth I was one of a hundred thousand people who marched from downtown San Francisco to a football stadium in Golden Gate Park where Mrs. Martin Luther King was one of the speakers. Two weeks later my father was watching his bowling ball roll away from him when he dropped dead of a heart attack. I returned to Nebraska for ten days.

****

Have you heard of Emmanuel Kant? He led Western civilization into a new world of thought, lived to be seventy-nine, yet never travelled more than ten miles from his place of birth. But for most of us physical detachment from "home" is a prerequisite for a mental one. Our leaving home in body is well-marked, usually a family event, sometimes even a community one, photographed and long-remembered and a scene beloved by novelists. But leaving home in mind is a private affair, un-recordable, rarely

41

mentioned, hardly ever discussed, and in my case I did not even know it had happened.

Five nights after my father's funeral I got together with old male friends from college (and one from high school) for an evening of poker. In the past I had had many such evenings with them and I was glad to see my old chums and at first it seemed just like old times. But after an hour or so I began to realize that I was no longer on the same wavelength as them. I know "wavelength" is a cliché, but I couldn't then and I still can't quite put my finger on it. It wasn't that they had come down in my estimation – because they hadn't. It was just that now the realm of experience to which my minute by minute consciousness related was more inclusive than theirs. This difference gave me a horrible feeling. When you leave home in body you can always, if you need to, go back. There may even be a dog there to wag its tail. But there was now no way I could ever get back to where my old friends around the table were. We were in different worlds now and I couldn't even explain it to them. By the evening's last hand I was in a state of concealed panic.

Back in Berkeley I woke from the same nightmare several nights a week. It came in variations, but the basic elements were always the same. I was alone, motor-less and oar-less, in a dingy drifting in the ocean but still close to the coast. A cliff ran along the shoreline and on its edge stood people from my Nebraska past, watching me drift out to sea. They were the variable element. Some nights it was my parents and twin sisters standing on the cliff's edge. Some nights it was my poker buddies. Some nights it was old girl friends. And some nights it was my former teachers, like Miss Porter my high school American history teacher who wanted me to follow my father into law. Some nights there were odd assortments gazing out at me. None of them ever shouted or even waved. Each dream ended when I had drifted so far out that I could no longer distinguish anyone on the cliff. Then I would wake up shouting and in a cold sweat.

Part Two: New World

My twin sisters departed for university when I was eight, and then, after flunking out, headed for Southern California. There they both married aeronautic engineers and settled on the same San Diego housing tract. Three months after my father died my mother sold the Puritan Avenue house and moved into a ranch house two minutes' drive from both my sisters. When summer school finished in early August I went down to give my mother support and to get acquainted with my sisters and my nieces and nephews and my brother-in-law's. I had intended to stay a month but my nightmares became more frequent and after two weeks I returned to Berkeley.

Meanwhile I had made two changes to my life. The first is boring but I need to tell you about it.

In June a meeting with my advisor went rather like the one I had with Professor Malonzo back in Lincoln. I had passed my comprehensive exams and would complete my course work at the end of summer school and I had already begun my dissertation, which, being no more than an extended mathematical exercise, I expected to finish by Christmas and to submit shortly thereafter. Its acceptance seemed highly probable. Even if I had to resubmit it once there would be time to receive my degree in June. I was exempt from the military draft because of a slight limp due to a hip damaged by polio the summer I was seven. So everything looked clear to my becoming an assistant professor somewhere in September '68.

My advisor confirmed that all this was 100 per cent plausible, but dangled in front of me another scenario. He suggested I maximize my chances of having a career in elite universities. To do so I should not submit my dissertation until my fourth year. Meanwhile I should try to have a couple of papers accepted by "top" journals and add a year of Berkeley teaching experience to my CV. He could arrange to have me appointed as an economics lecturer for my fourth year. He said that by doing it this way there was a good chance that I could begin my teaching career with a tenure-track job at an elite university.

I agreed.

The second change was that I moved out of the house with seven econ grad students and into a little dump of my own. I've lived in some nice abodes in my life, but with one exception, which I will tell you about later, I've loved none as much as this one. Why? Well I suppose mainly because it was my first. It had a split personality, half basement and half not and yet all on one level. A biology professor and his family lived overhead. The room I slept in, entertained in, studied in and something else I can't yet tell you about stretched across the width of the back of the

45

house. It felt twice the size a bedroom should be, and although furnished with all the basic stuff it seemed half-empty. The room's best features were two big windows looking onto a subtropical garden with flowers I had never, except in the movies, seen before. In front of one window I placed a small desk and in front of the other two wicker and metal chairs that looked like insects and between them a round plywood table with a built-in lamp. I especially liked being able to sit at my desk looking out at the garden.

My outside entrance door was at one end of the room. On the wall opposite the garden, a door led to the "basement". A half-step down and you were off the wooden floor of my bedroom and onto a concrete floor slopping toward a drain. There was a kitchen sink below a small window, a refrigerator older than me, an addition apparently made by my predecessor, a redwood picnic table with benches, a large furnace with shiny ducts and a flimsy plasterboard cubicle that housed a toilet and a shower but no wash basin.

I took occupancy the day I returned from San Diego. It was still August and my Berkeley was deserted, the sidewalks nearly pedestrian-free and the campus, except for maintenance crews, uninhabited. Somehow this emptiness gave rise inside me to a sensation of freedom. Even before my June meeting with my advisor I had entertained vague, dream-like thoughts about extending my social compass beyond economists. Occasionally I had even thought about extending the horizons of my mind beyond math and econ. Now with my new-found sensation of freedom and knowing that for a week at least I would be invisible to all who knew me, those dreams of venturing forth beyond my boundaries had unexpectedly become possibilities.

So where would I start?

Well, I've been holding something back. Remember Vanessa? And that package she handed me as we said goodbye in front of the British Museum? Well, I brought it with me to Berkeley, but I never opened it. I was afraid to open it. Partly because I was afraid of not making the grade at Berkeley and felt I needed to avoid distractions. But I think also because I was afraid those books, whatever they turned out to be, might lead me to some place I had in some way sworn not to go. In any case, back then there was not the time, I thought, to think of Vanessa-type-things. Then there was only the time to think of things that would lead me to a professor's chair.

But my second morning in my new pad I opened my steamer trunk and at the bottom found Vanessa's gift. The white tissue paper was crumpled, but the blue ribbon holding it together still had its bow. I pulled the ribbon and here is what I found.

> *Frank Lloyd Wright,* (I have forgotten the author)
> *O Pioneers,* by Willa Cather
> *The Great Gatsby*, by F. Scott Fitzgerald

The first two picks were easy to explain. Wright had been Vanessa's hero and exemplar of her new dream to design houses "intended not to glorify the rich and powerful but common folk like you and me." So it was natural for Vanessa to give me this picture book as a remembrance of her mind and soul. And *O Pioneers* is, as I surmised by

47

reading its back cover, a Nebraska book, the story of a family, like my grandmother's, that homesteaded on the open prairie. But it was not until later that day after I read its opening chapters that I saw why Vanessa had given me *The Great Gatsby*.

****

I now lived on the quiet, tree-shaded, half-professorial Northside. By foot the nearest campus entrance was eight minutes, the last block lined with shops: drugstore, butcher, grocer, cleaners, a three-screen arts cinema, a courtyard with two ethnic restaurants, two non-chain burger joints and just around the corner a laundromat and a large coffeehouse. The last soon became my new hangout. I've forgotten its real name, but I, like all its regulars, came to call it Enzo's after its friendly owner. And that morning after I opened Vanessa's package, I ventured into Enzo's – my first time in any of Berkeley's large coffeehouses. I carried my cappuccino out onto the empty covered front terrace, sat down at one of the marble-topped tables, took a deep breath and began reading *The Great Gatsby*.

Its narrator, a likeable young man, had just left the prairie, Minnesota this time, to begin a new life working in Manhattan and living on Long Island. Immediately he falls in with a fast, moneyed crowd, and the story tells how he does and does not cope with his new world. How thoughtful of Vanessa! But except for Sue Ruccio – economists don't count – I had not yet fallen in with anyone far removed from Puritan Avenue. Between Fitzgerald's chapters, I was mulling this over when a man of forty-plus wearing a plaid cap and a tweed jacket and jiggling an espresso cup and saucer sat down noisily at a table opposite. He made some remark about the weather, obviously intended as a conversation opener.

I ignored him. But his entrance into my field of vision on this auspicious morning had the immediate effect of bringing into the open thoughts that had been mouldering in my mind. According to *Time* I was living in control-central of a new generation or new culture – it was not sure which – of a kind unknown to human memory. This is the message that for two years I had at the weekend gleaned from the magazine's pages and more recently from *The Berkeley Barb.* Music, dress and hair-length were only sideshows. It was pot, peace and sex that were provoking the generational warfare, and in the beginning I had sided with my upbringing on all three. But a year of cannabis smoking (and one acid trip) had not diminished my ability and resolve to create and solve quadratic equations or to tie my shoes. And by now, like a quarter of the US population, I had come to realize that the war in Vietnam, the napalming and carpet-bombing of villages in particular, was un-American. As for sex, the most disturbing of all for the masses, I now had no difficulty with the idea that women no less than men should be allowed to enjoy it. Given my agreement on all three points and the fact that I was living at the epicenter – of whatever it was – I began to think that twenty-five years from then I might regret it if I had not participated in the revolution beyond the Be-In, a couple of peace marches and a number of orgasms. But here I now was, my first and overdue self-initiated venture into what I thought might be a source of *Time*'s agonies, and the only person in sight was a middle-aged Mr Uncool. *The Great Gatsby*, however, was giving me courage and after two chapters I decided to venture deeper.

I headed for the Southside and the two large coffeehouses in Telegraph Avenue's infamous 2400 block. Of course I had walked past them many times. The Forum, a former supermarket recently closed down by student shop-ins for refusing to employ blacks, was Parisian size. Just beyond its long street-side terrace was The Caffé Mediterraneum, or "The Med" as it was called. According to *Time*, Ginsberg had written *Howl* in it and Kerouac part of *On The Road*. Now despite it being August half the tables were occupied. If anyone had bothered to look, I would have stood out. I bought another cappuccino, and at a table under the mezzanine began Chapter Three.

****

That first week back in Berkeley in my new place, all alone and doing nothing in particular, but holding on to vague new dreams, was for me an unknown experience. If back then I had tried to explain the effect it was having on me I would have been hopelessly inarticulate. Nonetheless I did feel that maybe I was changing, not in the sense of who I was to the world, but changing in the sense of who I was to myself. For example, I began indulging simple pleasures. There were several tree-lined and pleasant ways you could walk from my place to Enzo's but my favourite was the way where some mornings I passed a woman who walked a monkey on a long yellow lead. Twice the monkey and I shook hands. With or without monkeys, mornings were now my favourite time and this time of year every morning was sunny and I always stopped at the drugstore at the top end of the shops on Euclid and bought a *San Francisco Chronicle*. At Enzo's I took my cappuccino and croissant out onto the terrace and read the *Chronicle* and slowly spooned the hot chocolaty foam and read the gossip columnist Herb Caen and watched the early morning coffee addicts coming and going. Afterwards I walked roundabout across the no-cars wooded campus, up Observation Hill, past Memorial Glade and the huge library, through Sather Gate, across Sproul Plaza, past Ludwig's Fountain (Ludwig was a dog) and the Student Union and then down Telegraph Avenue.

On my third day back in Berkeley I read more of *The Great Gatsby* sitting at an outside table at The Forum. I also got into cooking for myself. I acquired an electric frying pan and bought well-aged top round steak from Luke, my local butcher. The Med had a tiny Greek cafeteria at the back and for $1.04 you could have moussaka and salad, and for $1.09 rosemary chicken with zucchini and rice. I ate dinner there twice a week. The big coffee houses were getting more crowded now. People were returning, especially the grad students who made up fifty per cent of the 27,000 students. One evening eating pastitsio in The Med, I spotted Mario Savio and Jack Weinberg coming through the door. I recognized them because I had seen their photos in *Time*. Later that evening I finished *Gatsby*. At its end the book let me down badly. Nick, the narrator, became disillusioned with his new world and after a few months returned home, not just in body but also in mind. So I lost my identification with him and my nightmares continued.

****

Although for a whole week I frequented Berkeley's coffeehouses, by the end of the week I had met only one person. Guess who? Yes of course: Mr Uncool. And he was even more uncool than I had surmised on that first morning. He had the deepest southern accent I had ever heard.

"Do you mind if I join you?"

I did but I couldn't bring myself to say so. He sat down, bumping the table enough to slosh my cappuccino into the saucer. It was summer and, in addition to that plaid cap, he was wearing a tweed jacket from which he now pulled out a pipe. The state of its stem suggested it was more for chewing than for smoking. His hands weren't especially appealing either, heavily calloused and the nails rimmed with black. He said he repaired and maintained the presses of a large printer in Oakland and was on his way to work. But the really odd thing was that within five minutes I found myself enjoying Mr Uncool's company.

His real name was Calhoun Phifer. He had spent his first thirty-five years or so based in Mississippi and Louisiana, where he joined the merchant navy and for ten years or more worked out of New Orleans on steamers sailing up and down the coasts of Central and South America. Over time he worked himself up to the rank of first engineer. In his free time at sea he read about his ships' destinations, taught himself Spanish and in port ventured out on his own and explored. Somewhere along the way he must have gone to university because now he was working part-time on a masters in history at San Francisco State University. But a strange gap that. I mean between the Delta and Berkeley at thirty-five or thereabouts. And, as I was to learn, highly significant. Or so for a while I thought.

****

Across the street from The Med and The Forum were two large bookstores. Like the coffeehouses, they stayed open till late. Cody's, a new multi-story job, had large fiction and poetry sections, and the evening I finished *Gatsby*, mindful of what I had read in *Time*, I crossed over and bought *On The Road* and *Howl*.

A few doors away was Moe's, a large used book store that included a poster shop called The Print Mint. This brings me to a dimension of the counterculture that I haven't mentioned – graphic art. This shop-within-a-shop was Berkeley's main outlet for it. I had tried not to notice it. And I don't mean just this shop but the whole art movement that was emerging with such force from the Bay Area and whose images you by now saw everywhere, even on TV.

Why avoid it? Because at that point in my life, giving up painting and drawing so that I could have that Chevy was still the hardest thing I had ever done. In my late teens I had trained myself not even to look at art so as not to be tempted, because the deal was that if I reverted then Dad would take away my car. But I was 24 now, had no car to lose, and had not held a brush in my hand for eight years.

So that first week back in Berkeley I went into the Print Mint several times just to gaze. Then the day after I bought the Ginsberg and Kerouac books, I bought three posters for my pad and a couple of days later three more. I had identified several artists whose work I especially liked. Their medium was unfamiliar to me as it relied on color effects that could only be achieved with a lithographic printing press or by silk-screening.

****

Time *magazine, "Graphics: Nouveau Frisco"*

From coast to coast, be-ins, folk-rock festivals, art galleries and department-store sales are now advertised in posters and layouts done in a style that is beginning to be called Nouveau Frisco . . . . a vapor from the seething psychedelic dreamland of The Haight-Ashbury . . . .

****

from *Howl*, Allen Ginsberg

I'm addressing you.
Are you going to let your emotional life be run by
Time Magazine?
I'm obsessed by Time Magazine.
I read it every week.
Its cover stares at me every time I slink past the
corner candy store.

*I read it in the basement of the Berkeley Public
Library.
It's always telling me about responsibility.
Businessmen are serious. Movie producers are
serious. Everybody's serious but me.
It occurs to me that I am America.
I am talking to myself again.*

****

The thing – and please forgive me for what is going to
be a grandiose analogy – that has always seemed odd to
me about earthquakes is that nothing external to the Earth
causes them. The Earth is just there spinning around and
arching through space like it has for millions of years and
then suddenly some kind of internal contradiction activates
and the Earth starts to quake. It was sort of like that for me
when in September people returned and Berkeley life
resumed to normal.

All though September and beyond my enthusiasm for
my new abode and living arrangements continued. I was
glad to be living alone rather than with seven other guys,
and my daily walks through the leafy Northside and across
the carless campus continued to give me a kind of pleasure
that had not previously been mine. Now also nearly every
day my reading ventured beyond equations and their
explication. After finishing *The Great Gatsby* I read *Howl*,
On the Road, *O'Pioneers*, *Catcher in the Rye* and by mid-
October I was halfway through *Farewell to Arms*. I even
continued to eat Greek twice a week, and after those Med
dinners I twice ventured into art cinemas where I

experienced my first subtitles. Meanwhile I continued to be an economist. Although I was no longer going to classes and seminars, I spent time most days with my econ chums and twice on the weekends enjoyed the companionship of their visiting sisters. True, I now rarely spent time in my subterranean library carrel, but my dissertation was progressing faster than I had hoped and I had started a paper with the idea of submitting it to a journal.

So everything seemed and really was going my way. Even my recurring nightmares had ceased. Anyone, including myself, would have said that Mike Hope's existence had never looked so manageable, so desirable and its future so assured. I was spinning effortlessly and on course through life. But inside me something was beginning to happen; I was beginning to quake. Increasingly it seemed there were two *mes* and there was slippage between them. There was the Mike Hope who reduced human reality to equations and dreamed of being called "Professor", and there was the Mike Hope who had seen two Truffaut movies and wanted to see more and who identified with Holden Caulfield. It was the slippage between myself and myself that now occasionally made me quake. It was like my inner being started to tremble, and although these existential quakes only lasted a minute or three and only when I was alone and unoccupied, I worried about them. Twice I had bad quakes when sitting alone at Enzo's and then one morning I thought I was about to have a third. I was sitting with a cappuccino at a table on the terrace, watching the passing morning life when suddenly and to my great relief Calhoun, Mr Uncool, appeared. As always he was wearing his plaid cap.

By now Calhoun and I had gotten into the habit of meeting accidentally a couple mornings a week at Enzo's. At first I had tried to find out how he came to leave the Deep South when he did, but when it became clear he didn't want to talk about that I dropped it. The third or fourth time we met he invited me to come around to his house. He said he owned and lived in a Berkeley house with two other bachelors and that every Friday people stopped by after work, sometimes not many in which case they might go out for a pizza. But other times lots turned up and stayed late. I thanked him for the invites and made excuses why I couldn't come.

I no longer thought about how uncool Calhoun was because I so enjoyed talking with him. Being in conversation with Calhoun was like riding a rollercoaster that wasn't scary. He had a thousand stories to tell and shelves of books to draw upon, but what he most liked talking about were the peculiarities of everyday people like you, me and himself. Calhoun and I were not yet quite friends, but on that morning our acquaintanceship deepened. I was always glad to see Calhoun but, as you can imagine, especially so on that morning. He sat down, rocking the table, apologized for being clumsy and took off his cap. I can't remember how our conversation began but for twenty minutes it rolled effortlessly up and down and around surprising bends and this relaxed me and by now I was feeling happy and then somehow – for the first time ever in California – I let drop that I used to be serious about painting.

Calhoun slammed the palm of his hand down on the table.

"THAT'S IT!"

"What's it?"

"YOU!"

"Me? What about me?"

"I've been trying to figure you out for months and now I have."

"What the hell are you talking about, Calhoun?"

"I'll try to explain."

I waited for him to find his pipe. He looked ridiculously pleased with himself.

"I could never quite make you add up. You never indicated that you had any serious interests other than mathematics and maybe women. If you'll forgive me for saying so, you aren't even well-read for your age, and yet I always got the feeling that there was another important dimension to you. And I was right. You're an artist."

"Bullshit. I haven't done any art since I was fifteen. My father promised me a car for my sixteenth if I gave it up. And I did. Completely."

"But the artist is still inside you, influencing you, making you react to life in ways that you wouldn't if you were just an economist."

"Bull." I shook my head.

"Your father wouldn't have made such a big deal of it if you hadn't been serious about your art. You WERE serious, weren't you?"

"What difference does it make?"

"I'm trying to get to know you."

"It's not who I am now."

"Maybe so, but can you tell me a little about it anyway?"

"Like what?"

"Like how old were you when you started?"

"I can't remember."

"Ten? Eleven?"

"Earlier than that."

"How early?"

"I don't know, but by the time I was seven or eight teachers at school were telling me that I had talent."

"And did you do art out of school?"

"All the time. By eight I was doing watercolours and by ten I was selling them in church art fairs. I'd tell people that my mother had painted them and I was selling them for her. Later I got into acrylics and still later into oils. In our basement I set up a little studio where I didn't have to worry about dripping paint."

"Did you have instruction?"

"A little. There was a local artist, Mr Frazer, who was the best painter in town and he sort of took me under his wing for a while. But when I was fourteen he moved to Ohio. I mostly stopped. Then my mother's sister came to visit. She had lived in New York City and Washington D C and was rather sophisticated. She made me show her lots of my work and then the next day she came back from downtown with a big book of Matisse's paintings for me. You know his work?"

"A bit."

"Well, I went crazy about it. I started painting and drawing more than ever and I think that's when my father started to get really worried about it."

Calhoun looked at his watch.

"Listen Mike. I'm terribly sorry but I've got to go. A press broke down and I promised to be there twenty minutes ago. I want you to do two things for me."

He fumbled in the pockets of his tweed jacket. Eventually he pulled out a little dog-eared notebook, tore out a sheet on which he wrote some things, folded it and handed it to me.

"First, I want you to take and keep this. It's my address. Second, as you know, I've invited you at least twice to come around on Fridays. Why don't you come this Friday? Think about it. You might enjoy yourself more than you think. I've got to rush now. It's been wonderful to get to know you finally."

For some reason Calhoun was laughing now. When he got up from the table I forgot to grab hold of my cup. It rolled around but was empty. When I looked up he was out of sight. I could hardly believe that I had told him about my art. I had never told anyone.

****

Friday came and I decided to go to Calhoun's place. I waited till six to head out. It was a long walk, a couple of miles and down near the train tracks that separated white Berkeley from black. It was dark on Berkeley Way as I approached. Through the picture window of the small house I saw people standing with drinks in their hands. The front door, up a half flight of steps, was wide open and I stepped into a small entrance hall. A couple standing in the doorway to the front room turned to look at me. They were a handsome pair, he in his mid-thirties, she maybe a decade younger and wearing a sheik, tight-fitting lavender dress.

"Don't be shy. We'll protect you," said the man.

"He knows karate and I have a magic wand," she said.

Their friendly tease put me at ease.

"Thanks, the magic wand should be especially useful. What do you see as the greatest danger?"

"This must be him," she said to her companion.

"Obviously."

"Obviously what?"

"We know all about you."

"Impossible."

"We got here early and Calhoun told us about you. He said to be on the lookout for a young man with a cowboy accent."

"For God's sake, what a way to be known."

"He says you're an artist disguised as an economist."

"Calhoun got a bit carried away by a story I told him."

"It's a lovely story," she said.

"Shit. I never told anyone about my secret past and now everyone knows, even complete strangers."

"Not strangers for long, I hope. This is Loraine and I'm John Gerassi. My friends call me Tito."

"I'm . . . well I suppose you know my name."

"Yes, Mike," she said and I shook hands with them both.

"Are either of *you* in disguise?"

"I wish I were," said Gerassi. "I'm a history professor at San Francisco State, and if I had more artistic talent I'd be off to Paris tomorrow."

"Why Paris?"

"I suppose because I was born there and my father was an artist there."

"Wow, but then I was pretty sure you weren't a cowboy."

That got a laugh. As we manoeuvred our way into the front room Calhoun spotted me and came lunging toward us.

"It was a struggle but we captured him, Calhoun," said Gerassi.

"I'm going to take him away before he escapes. I want him to meet Simon. I'm so glad you came, Mike. Follow me."

The place was heterogeneously packed. We squeezed our way into a second room, through it and into a big kitchen crowded with a mixture of academic and arty types. Calhoun led me up to one of the latter, a man pushing forty leaning against the fridge.

"This is Mike Hope, the guy I was telling you about. Mike, this is Simon."

Simon's self-presentation, even ignoring the bellbottoms, was not what I was used to. Tall, thin and slightly stooped, he had a long pinched face with a long blond beard that tapered for several miles before ending in a point just above his studded belt. Offsetting his beard was a matching ponytail. His thin-lipped mouth was nearly expressionless, but his blue eyes kept twinkling and when we shook hands his silver and copper bracelets – at least a dozen – jangled.

"I'm afraid Calhoun has kept you a secret," I said.

"Calhoun has a lot of secrets," said Simon

"Simon is one of the two guys I own this house with and he works in graphic art."

"I didn't think you were a banker."

"Simon laughed. "I'm a librarian of sorts."

"He used to be," interjected Calhoun.

"I used to drive a mobile library van around to the little towns the other side of the hills. Then the psychedelic poster thing started."

"And?"

"And a couple of my artist friends thought of turning some of their stuff into posters. So I ended up starting a poster company."

"And?"

"And when it took off I packed in the mobile library thing. This" – he was looking at the long-haired man my age or younger with whom he had been talking as we approached, "is one of my artist friends, John Thompson."

"John Thompson? The John Thompson who did the *Flower Child* poster?"

"I did the drawing; Simon chose the color."

"I've got it on my wall!"

Thompson was visibly pleased by this and we shook hands.

"How's it done? I've tried to figure it out, but can't."

"There's a copy of it in the library," said Simon. "Come with us and we'll show you."

In the dining room a slender, straight-backed young woman in a white mini and with an expensive looking green leather handbag hanging from her shoulder stood in our path. She stepped back to let us through. As she turned, our eyes met and momentarily locked. If I had been free I would have stopped and tried to make her acquaintance.

Instead I followed Simon and John into a room with two walls lined with books. On a third wall hung ten or twelve psychedelic posters, one of them *Flower Child*[3]. Years later it occupied the back cover of Thames and Hudson's *The History of Posters*. Viewing it on a wall from a distance you see only the outlines of a young woman's face with blue eyes peering through a mass of brilliant green dotted with blue. A closer look reveals that the green is thousands of inter-looping strands of hair entwined with hundreds of tiny blue-petalled flowers with orange centers. It was the combination of the massive intensity of flat color with the fine-lined delicacy of detail that compelled me to buy it when I saw it in The Print Mint.

Simon and John explained to me how such a poster is created. Of course its most important element was its first, John's black and white, pen and ink drawing. But having once been a colorist of sorts, I wanted to know how the color effects had been achieved. Simon and John explained that they came from doing the color separations by hand rather than by camera and by laying on the ink extremely thick.

They described all this to me in detail, including showing me overlays and printing plates which Simon retrieved from a closet. Meanwhile the door to the crowded dining room remained open and several times I noticed flashes of light, presumably from someone taking pictures. But I was so absorbed I never looked around to see who he or she was or what the object of their interest was. Once the light

[3] http://www.smith.edu/artmuseum/On-View/Past-Exhibitions/Summer-of-Love/Counterculture/Counterculture-Posters

flashed closer, as if the photographer had moved into our room.

Each answer to my questions about the posters led to new ones, and I don't know how much time passed before I turned my attention to Simon and John. They had not only indulged me, they had also taught me a lot. Simon, whose mouth seemed rarely to smile but when it did revealed unusually beautiful teeth, looked faintly amused. John, I think, was flattered by the interest I had shown.

"Have you been drawing a long time?" I asked him.

"As long as I can remember."

"Were your parents supportive?"

"Well yes, they paid for me to study art at university. I graduated in June from Davis." By "Davis" he meant the University of California at Davis.

"Are *they* artists?"

"My mother decorates cakes and my father has a flower garden. He's also a Bank of America executive."

"And *he* looks like a banker," said Simon, his eyes laughing. "I met him last week."

At that point someone entered the room and ended our conversation. A few minutes later I re-emerged into the larger party. It was still going strong. I had not forgotten the woman in the white mini with the green leather handbag with whom I had exchanged meaningful glances. Thinking of what Vanesa had said to me the night we met, I searched in all the rooms for her but she had gone. I stayed another hour and met a number of people who on any other night of my life up to then would have won a permanent place in my memory. But, with the one fleeting exception, my half hour with Simon, John and *Flower Child* reduced all of my other social exchanges that evening to insignificance.

****

Physical self-mutilation is not the worst kind of self-mutilation. When you are young and you are doing the worst kind, you may not, unlike with the physical kind, even know you are doing it. In exchange for a Chevy I had, unknown to myself, amputated my soul or at least my means of communicating with it. For me the means of communicating was my painting and my drawing, but for other people the means can be any of millions of things and even many things at the same time. But those thoughts only came to me much later. That night during my long walk home alone in the dark after my first visit to Berkeley Way my thoughts were more confused than I could ever remember them being. And of course that confusion was a good and healthy sign. It lasted half the night and all the next day and then half the night again and then Sunday lunchtime I made a big decision.

Monday morning I went to my bank, withdrew one hundred dollars and then spent it all in an artist supply shop on Telegraph Avenue. That afternoon I turned half my oversized bedroom into a studio. I moved my insect-like chairs and table to the side with my bed and desk. In front of the now empty window looking onto the garden I placed my new easel and next to it a Formica kitchen table that had been hiding under a half inch of dust behind the furnace. Then I laid down some rules.

1. Monday through Friday no painting or drawing until I had done at least six hours of economics.
2. I would never put any art material or work on my desk.
3. I would not tell my fellow grad students or any professors (some were now seeking my mathematical advice on this or that) about the new dimension to my life.
4. Before leaving my place I would always check that there was no paint or ink on my hands and clothes.

So there I was, finally. Sue had cut open my cocoon; Calhoun had persuaded me to stick my head out, and now, after Simon and John's tutorial, I had crawled free. I was not on my feet yet and in my head I was definitely not fully healthy yet, but I was not middle-aged anymore and maybe even on the verge of discovering my youth. Meanwhile all around me the past was exploding. No one appreciated this more than *Time*. Week after week I read its accounts of happenings in Berkeley and San Francisco:

> *"one simply cannot escape the conclusion that we are confronting a new culture . . . . First it was free speech, then filthy speech. Now it is free love . . . students and nonstudents continue to test the limits of the permissible at Berkeley . . . . The Berkeley Free Sex movement contends man will only become free when society stops trying to manage his sex life for him. . . . The Haight-Ashbury has become over the past year the center of a new utopianism, compounded of drugs and dreams,*

*free love and LSD . . . . Their professed aim is
nothing less than the subversion of Western society
. . . . Tourist buses have already made The Haight-
Ashbury a regular stop. . . . the sickly scent of
incense fills the air to mask the reek of marijuana . .
. . now that the psychedelic revolution is really
under way, they are discovering new highs with
dizzying speed . . . . The drummer roars back with
a thumping beat. The guitarists twang away lustily.
And, momentum building, voices wailing and
systems gogo, The Jefferson Airplane blasts off . .
. . the hottest new rock group in the country . . . .
the anointed purveyor of the San Francisco Sound .
. . . Today, hippie enclaves are blooming in every
major U.S. city from Boston to Seattle, from Detroit
to New Orleans . . . . There are outposts in Paris
and London, New Delhi and Katmandu . . . . They
are predominantly white, middleclass, educated
youths overendowed with all the qualities that make
their generation so engaging, perplexing and
infuriating . . . . Above all as New York's Senator
Robert Kennedy puts it: 'They want to be
recognized as individuals, but individuals play a
smaller and smaller role in society.'"*

And it was not just *Time*. We were the first television
generation. Videotape had just been invented and
beginning with the Human Be-In unedited videotape images
of rebellion were being disseminated across continents and
oceans as they happened. Day by day the whole world

watched a generation rebel against racism, sexism, war, imperialism and puritanism.

****

I was hoping the woman with the green leather handbag would be at Calhoun's when I returned to Berkeley Way and the salon the following Friday. But fewer people were there than on my first Friday and she wasn't one of them. John Thompson, however, the *Flower Child* artist, was there, and my social confidence shot up when he seemed genuinely glad to see me again. It shot up even more when he suggested we meet up sometime in the coming week.

Gerassi, or Tito as he called himself, was also there. He took to calling me the Cowboy and I might have found a way of returning the compliment if I had not suspected that behind this unflattering label and the sardonic smiles he harboured good feelings towards me. In a three-way with Calhoun he said, "What the Cowboy needs is a wife. Maybe I can find him one." Naturally I thought he was joking.

****

On Thursday of that week I had just finished dinner when John Thompson phoned. We agreed to meet at The Forum at ten that evening.

It was November now and some days it rained but that night when I stepped outdoors it was dry and warm and when I looked up at the sky I saw the stars. I'd been cooped up indoors all day, first at my desk and then, after

John phoned, at my easel. So now it felt especially good to be out walking in the night air and walking along Euclid with other young people doing the same.

The bells up in the Campanile sounded the hour as I walked under the great arch of Sather Gate and into Sproul Plaza. The huge plaza was dark and, except for a couple sitting on the edge of the fountain, deserted. In front of me Telegraph Avenue's lights shimmered in the near distance as I hurried across the plaza, passed the Student Union and came out onto the Avenue. On the first corner a Bob Dylan busker was performing "It's Alright Ma (I'm Only Bleeding)". He had a crowd around him, and people were dropping coins in his guitar case. I passed a bearded leafleteer, then a Great Dane on a lead and then three co-eds standing in front of a blue-lighted boutique window looking in at ebony mannequins dressed in long-sleeved white mini-dresses. All along the Avenue the sidewalks were busy with walkers. I passed the Chinese cafeteria, the artist supply shop, the Avenue's two art cinemas, the French patisserie and then the little headshop with its flashing strobe. Graffiti on the front of the Bank of America branch said FEELING IS GOOD FOR YOU. I reached the 24-hundred block and the sidewalks were crowded. It was a virtual orgy of perambulation and all you could hear was the hum of conversations. Cody's and Moe's were still open, and the Forum's long terrace was packed. I spotted John at the far end. He had secured a table next to the sidewalk. I congratulated him and then went inside and up to the green marble-topped bar and ordered a pineapple frappé for me and a latte for John.

It was one of those evenings that warm the heart and make you feel that the world is a kindly uplifting place and that you know where you are going. And although I don't remember much about our conversation that evening, the feel of being there still lives inside me. John, always modest and soft-spoken, had only been in Berkeley four months but already he seemed part of the scene. He mentioned Wilson, Mososco, Beck, Crumb, Sätty and Bowen as artists he had met. Except for Sätty, one of whose posters was thumb-tacked to my wall, the names meant nothing to me. I asked John about his wife. I had yet to meet her. Simon, who I now knew was gay, said she was adorable.

"She would have come tonight," John explained, "but she has an exam tomorrow, her first since transferring from Davis."

A *Berkeley Barb* vendor, my age, appeared on the terrace going table to table. John seemed to know him. We both bought a copy.

"I sold *Barbs* the third month I was here. That's how I know that guy."

"Did you make any money?"

"I didn't get rich but if you time it right it's not bad money considering what it is. The secret is to be over on Oregon Street when the printer's van from San Francisco delivers the new issue on Thursday nights about nine-thirty or ten."

"Like a few minutes ago".

"Yah, and then you rush down here and to The Med. I used to sell fifty copies within half an hour. Then I'd rush back for fifty more. The second fifty might take me an hour to unload. Then I'd get fifty more and head for home and sell another fifteen or twenty on the way. In the morning Gwen, that's my wife, would sell the others while walking to class."

"And how much did you make?"

"You buy them for ten cents and sell them for twenty. So we'd make fifteen dollars. Our rent is sixty dollars a month. So that was a week's rent."

"Or fourteen dinners at The Med."

"Yah, not bad for less than three hours work. Maybe I should start doing it again."

We chatted about this and that, but mostly about being an artist or rather about John being an artist. He told me where to buy materials – not the shop I had gone to – about the different poster publishers and which artists were the movement's leaders. He also had some gossip about them. It was good sitting there chatting with John and sometimes we just watched the people going by. Every few minutes a tall muscular black man in a blond wig and a strapless pink dress with a micro skirt that flared out like a Swan Lake ballerina's strolled by, hips swinging, arms flapping, nose pointing to the stars. People pretended not to notice. Across the street a long-haired young man wearing a top hat walked back and forth between Moe's and Cody's waving a placard reading "Be Young and Be Quiet".

"Do you realize," asked John, "how lucky we are to be young now and here?"

"I'm beginning to."

We finished our drinks and John went up to the bar. The *Barb*'s want ads were usually good for a laugh or two, so I had a look.

Two attractive young women with nice Berkeley flat need handsome and virile man to provide daily sexual satisfaction and prepare and serve breakfast and dinner. $30 per week plus board and room. For an interview call - - - - - - - .

John returned with two plates of cheese cake. For the umpteenth time the transvestite pranced past but this time two paces behind him marched "Be Young and Be Quiet" from across the street. People laughed. A few minutes later the pair returned skipping arm-in-arm and the terrace roared. The two skippers looked delighted, especially the ballerina.

About midnight John and I said goodbye and headed home in opposite directions.

****

Part of the enchantment of being young is that you do not yet put everyone you meet into neat little categories. This enables you to experience people as individuals to a degree that will be beyond your powers when you are older and "sophisticated". But even today, the third co-owner of Calhoun's house escapes my powers of categorization. He was the person who on my first visit to Berkeley Way entered the library, ending my conversation about poster-art. Tall, overweight and thirty-plus, he stood there in the doorway in a double-breasted, dark blue suit that suggested both a 1940s matinée idol and a bargain from

Goodwill. Glimmers of lamplight reflected off his thick horn-rimmed glasses.

"Mike," said Simon, "this is Alan the third owner of this house. Alan, this is the economist that Calhoun was talking about. We are trying to persuade him to give it up in favour of art."

"Don't listen to these guys. They'll screw you up."

I couldn't tell if he was serious or joking.

"Don't listen to Calhoun either."

"Who should I listen to?"

"Don't listen to anybody, especially not me," he chuckled. "But you should come here every Friday. We'll chat sometime."

With that he had lumbered out of the room.

The following Friday I didn't see Alan again at Berkeley Way. But then on Sunday morning I was sitting alone on the terrace at Enzo's fantasizing about becoming a painter, when to my right the door of the coffee house opened and Alan walked out. I invited him to join me. He sat down with his cup and saucer and I set about trying to find out more about him.

"Tell me, Calhoun is a mechanic and part-time graduate student; Simon is an ex-librarian turned poster producer. What about you?"

"I'm a draughtsman and a part-time architecture student." As he spoke he removed his horn-rims and began wiping the lenses with a large white handkerchief.

"Here at Berkeley?"

"Yes." He held his glasses up high so as to see the lenses better. "I work up . . . " He stopped talking to blow on each lens. ". . . the hill at Lawrence Laboratory. I've been working on the architecture degree for ages, but it looks like I'll get it in June."

Following an awkward exchange of comments on a passing young woman, Alan began telling what was obviously going to be a long story.

"A few years ago," he began, "after work I came through that door with a glass of wine looking for a table on this terrace. But they were all occupied. Then this young woman – and I immediately took in how attractive she was – popped into view. She was sitting at that table and facing the door, and then, low and behold, she smiled at me and pointed at the empty chair facing her. Well of course I accepted and sat down. We started talking, and immediately we felt comfortable and relaxed with each other, and time passed, and then she remembered to look at her watch. 'Oh my God, she said, I've got to pick up Johnnie.' Well, it turned out Johnnie was her four-year old son and the two of them lived near here. And then she invited me home for dinner. Well of course I accepted. You would've too, if you'd seen her. And then . . . ."

Alan paused for a sip of espresso.

"After she put Johnnie to bed, we ate dinner by candlelight, and after I helped her clean-up we went to bed. And she was wonderful in bed, really wonderful. In the morning she invited me back for the coming night and then on the next morning the same again. But on the third morning she invited me to move in with them. Well, I couldn't do that. I just couldn't. And I felt really bad about it."

That seemed to be the end of the story.

"Well, did you ever see her again?"

"No, and I stayed away from here for over a year. Such is life. Pretty fucked up really."

End of story. And I didn't know what to make of it. On the one hand I thought he had made it up. I couldn't imagine him attracting women in the magnetic way his story implied. I couldn't even imagine him having much of any attraction given his appearance and manner. But even so his telling of the story had charmed me. His voice was rich and mellow and his flow of words smooth and dream-inducing, and at the end of it I found myself actively liking Alan. Why? I asked myself then and now again. Because, I think, he had told the story without any perceptible trace of egotism, something few men could do with such a story about themselves, be it true or false.

A few days later I was walking with Calhoun across campus.

"Sunday I ran into your housemate Alan at Enzo's."

"Yah, he told me."

"And he told me a story."

"Alan is always telling stories."

"It was a story about an attractive woman picking him up and taking him home to bed."

"That sounds like an Alan story."

"You mean he goes around telling stories like that?"

Calhoun laughed. "Oh of course, you thought it was bullshit."

"You mean it wasn't?"

"Alan never bullshits. He's constitutionally incapable of it."

Calhoun was clearly amused by my incredulity.

"He's a ladies' man?"

"A steady stream of twenty-two-year-olds seem to find him irresistible."

"You're joking."

"It's hard to believe, I know."

"Christ, how does he do it?"

"He's too laid back to do anything. He just waits for them to come to him."

"I don't believe it."

"I didn't either at first. Then he had the first of his annual parties for the girls he's currently sleeping with. Seven came."

"My God, what's his secret?"

"If I knew, I'd be using it."

****

Near the bottom of University Avenue was a bodega. Of course it was not called a bodega but it was like a bodega in that you could take in bottles, and from big barrels they would fill your bottles with wine. After I moved into my own pad I got into the habit of going down to the bodega once a month to fill a gallon jug with California red. I kept the jug next to the furnace on the redwood picnic table where most nights I ate dinner alone. It could not have been very good wine, but I liked it a lot and always had a glass or two with my dinner.

****

"The secret book in the secret place." That is how Simon described it to me that Friday evening as people were beginning to arrive for the salon. We were talking about color. I needed to know more about color, and had decided Simon knew more than me.

"Have you heard of Josef Albers?" he asked.

"I've heard the name."

"He was a member of the Bauhaus, and after he escaped from the Nazis he ended up on the faculty at Yale. Albers is interested in color, color and color. He has built his whole career on the study of color. He is especially interested in how colors interact. I presume you've noticed that the colors in Mososco's posters interact."

"Of course." I had checked Mososco out at the Print Mint after my conversation with John at The Forum.

"Well, Mososco studied under Albers at Yale. And that brings me to a sort of secret, a double secret: a secret book in a secret place." Simon obviously liked that last phrase.

"Albers' crowning achievement," he continued, "is a silk-screened book titled *The Interaction of Color*. It consists of about 150 prints. They only printed a hundred or so copies because as you can imagine it cost a fortune to silk-screen. And now because there are so few copies and because Albers is famous it's worth a quadruple fortune. And one of those copies lives here in Berkeley."

"Where?"

"It's owned by the university. But they don't like people to know about it because it is too valuable to be handled much or even at all. But it was donated to the university as a library book, and so they have to let you look at it if you find out about it."

"You've seen it and held it in your hands, then?

"It's too fucking big to hold in your hands." Simon laughed and tugged on the long end of his beard, his bracelets jangling. He was delighted with the effect his story was having on me.

"Alright, where do I go and how do I persuade them to let me look at it?"

****

As I think I said before, there were no cars on the Berkeley campus, just people and trees and paved pathways curving through the green spaces between the buildings and you could walk and walk without thinking about cars. And another peculiarity for me from the flatlands was that the whole campus was on a slope. From halfway down, the slope was gentle but up toward the top where the campus began in the foothills the slope was steep and as you walked up you felt the steepness in your legs. Two small streams, both called Strawberry Creek, South Fork and North Fork, came down out of the hills and trickled down through the campus, except in the winter when sometimes they cascaded. The South Fork of Strawberry Creek was the clue Simon gave me for finding the secret place.

Before that chat with Simon I had never heard of the "Art Gallery". I found it, a squat stone building tucked between bigger buildings and surrounded by trees and shrubs and on one side bordered by Strawberry Creek. It had just gone two. No one was about. I crossed over the creek on a wooden footbridge and under towering eucalyptuses came up to the tiny gallery and its massive wooden door.

An Indian woman wearing a yellow sari directed me into a small unoccupied room opposite the reception desk and told me to wait. Two glass walls looked over the green banks of the creek and into woods with patches of sunlight. I sat down on the room's only chair and leaned forward on a large oak table and gazed out at the trees and the ferns growing along the creek. I was already in heaven when an oldish man entered struggling with the biggest book I had ever seen. He laid it carefully down on the table in front of me. Then he turned and from close-range looked me in the eyes. I thanked him, but he said nothing and turned away and closed the door softly behind him.

That was my first of many visits to the secret place.

After my second visit when leaving I followed a path up the slope. I didn't know where the path was leading me but walking in the light of the late October afternoon and with the sun low in a blue sky, made me feel happy. I walked around a bend and further up the slope and came onto an oval expanse of lawn surrounded by trees. The trees were enormous. The sunlight filtered down through the leafy branches, laying waving streaks of gold across the deep green of the lawn. But it was the dogs that grabbed my attention. A dozen dogs of assorted sizes, shapes and colours were racing around, frolicking, sometimes in threes and fours, sometimes all in one noisy gang. There had been many such dogs in my childhood. My father's love of his lawn kept me from having a dog of my own and I had made up for it by making friends with all the free-roaming dogs in my neighbourhood.

I sat down on the grass and watched the Berkeley dogs. Other people were scattered around the perimeter, sort of a dog theatre-in-the-round, doing the same. There was a Dalmatian, a brown boxer, a toy collie, a spanielesk mongrel and other mongrels of more obscure origins. An overweight black Labrador with a blue ball in her mouth meandered in slow motion between the other dogs. A knee-high mongrel with shaggy brown and white fur was tantalizing its peers by waving a long stick clamped in its jaws. The boxer, when he was not strutting about trying to get the attention of a long-haired dachshund, demonstrated his masculinity by repeatedly taking well-aimed pees. Meanwhile the Dalmatian started humping the collie, and a big red terrier chased a tiny black and white terrier who was chasing the big shaggy mongrel with the stick.

After watching their soap opera for a while I noticed a twist in the plot. One of the dogs, a male, appeared half-wild. And it was not just that he looked like a coyote. It was also that, unlike the other dogs, he appeared to maintain a psychological distance, if not from the opera itself, then at least from its silliness. When the boxer and the big red terrier became boisterous, someone to my right shouted "Descartes, Descartes". I turned and saw a girl about my age sitting nearby on the grass. The coyote – he had to be at least half coyote – broke from the group and sauntered toward the girl and then nuzzled her pretty face as she stroked him. She whispered a few words and then he returned to the stage. Now I was more interested in the girl than the coyote. She was small, slight, dark-haired and looked as wild as Descartes. I tried to make eye contact but she pretended not to notice. A few minutes later she stood up, called Descartes and they left.

Crossing Strawberry Creek on my way back to my flat I started thinking again about the woman with the green leather handbag I had made eye contact with my first night at the salon. That – "the woman with green leather handbag" – was the ridiculous name I had given her. But what struck me as more ridiculous was that I kept, periodically I mean, thinking of her. Our contact, purely with the eyes, had been less than ten seconds and now nearly four weeks had passed and that sub-ten-second memory kept flashing in my mind. If she had been beautiful or visually striking in some other way then my brain waves might have been forgiven. But she was not, as must be obvious given my inability to offer you any strong image of her other than a fucking handbag.

****

Another little episode developed out of my Friday evenings at the salon. At first it seemed of no significance. Gerassi, the debonair thirty-something who had told me not to be afraid when I was crossing the Berkeley Way threshold for the first time, got it into his head that I needed a wife. This re-emerged on our third meeting, and began with a bit of bad humour on my part. Instead of calling me The Cowboy, which I hated, he began calling me Nebraska, only a slight improvement. When I communicated my lack of amusement, his playful blond sidekick, who always wore a lavender dress but never the same one, jumped in.

"Your name change is a sign that you are coming up in the world."

"At this rate I'll make the cover of *Time* by Easter."

"Gerassi," said Calhoun, "used to be an editor at *Time*."

"Bull."

"I'm afraid it's true," said Gerassi.

"THE *Time*?"

"Fraid so. And *Newsweek* also."

Calhoun's face told me I was being told the truth.

"But I do better and more important things now, like finding you a wife."

I laughed nervously.

"I'm serious. We're having a small party next Saturday night. Ostensibly it will just be a party, but I've picked out three eligible young ladies for you to choose from. All clever and attractive."

It was a ridiculous idea of course, but possibly amusing. Calhoun drove me; and Alan and Simon came along. Gerassi lived in a brand-new flat in Pacific Heights, a San Francisco neighbourhood as posh as its name suggests. As soon as we arrived he introduced me to the three candidates, all law students. One I rather took to – I even spent some time alone with her in a darkened room – and if I had not been infected with green-handbag thoughts something more serious might have developed. But on the night – it was alcohol based – the only thing that made an impression on me was what happened at the short end of the L-shaped living room. There by itself and cut off from the flow was a deep arm chair. Alan spotted it when we arrived and occupied it immediately. At the end of the evening he was still there but no longer alone. One of my would-be wives was sitting on an arm of his chair and the other two on the floor at his feet. He was telling them stories.

****

A few days later Simon rang when I was finishing dinner. He said he and John Thompson were nearby and that if it was alright with me they would stop by for a few minutes just to say hello. Of course I said yes. It was only when I hung up that it dawned on me that their real reason for dropping in was to check out my painting.

I was a bit nervous. I offered them wine but they turned it down in favour of the joint that Simon, wearing even more bracelets than usual, was already rolling. I showed then most of what I had painted in the last month and explained what I was doing and where I thought I needed to improve my technique, especially with color. Simon, whose beard and ponytail seemed longer than ever, gave nothing away, but John was clearly impressed. They stayed about an hour. On their way out Simon, who had still not said a word about my work, turned to face me, his mouth serious, but his eyes twinkling.

"A couple of those with the appropriate caption would make excellent posters. I guess you know where to find me."

****

I have been telling you mostly about the new quasi-bohemian side to my life because, besides being more important to my story, it is what gives me more pleasure to remember. But I was still a committed econ grad student. Monday to Friday I got in six hours a day at it and usually lunched with economists. I still planed not to submit for another year, but my dissertation was already nearing the halfway point. The truth is I enjoyed the hard concentration of doing math, although now not as much as painting. With the coming of November the days grew shorter and darker and the mornings were now often wet and chilly. My big split-personality room was not exactly cosy, but it was warm and I still liked my half-basement flat as much as when I moved in. But sometimes now I did have a problem with it. In my first two Berkeley years I had not, except for those seven summer weeks seeing Sue Ruccio on the sly, been close to anyone. Through my studies I had made lots of what in common usage are called "friends", and my relations with my opposite sex had not always been chaste. But I had not – and I hesitate to use this word – bonded with any of them. This of course is a criticism of me, not of them. As the no-family, no-ties careerist that I was, life reduced to a matter of ends and means. I had not decided to make it like that; I had not even thought about it, but as with a lot of people it had just happened. Calhoun was its saboteur. Now I found myself living a life I had not sought nor even imagined. There would never be a Professor Malonzo to spell out its possibilities. Mine was no longer that kind of life and now with the salvation came loneliness. Not overpowering surges of it but whispers from the corners of my room, in the evenings mostly, sometimes as I stood at my easel.

****

When I arrived at Berkeley Way the Friday following Simon and John's visit, Simon invited me to "come below". As with many Berkeley and San Francisco houses "below" was at ground level and at its back was Simon's bedroom looking onto the rear garden. But the rest of "below" was occupied by his business: shelves loaded with thousands of posters, tables for packing orders, a studio with a light table, and an office. Simon showed me around and he talked shop. He told me which of my paintings interested him and how I should proceed. He even explained royalties.

When I came up from below I got to chatting with a young anthropologist. He had just returned from fieldwork in New Guinea and was enthusiastically detailing to me the sexual practices of what he called "my tribe" when suddenly from the front room I heard a woman's voice say, "I'm not a fast food and fast sex sort of person."

It was not a loud voice but a voice projected like a stage actor's voice, and I moved slightly to my left so as to see the voice's owner. To my amazement it was her. She even had the same green leather bag hanging from her shoulder. Her lime green dress, tight-fitting and two shades lighter than her handbag, was too long to qualify as a mini but only by the width of a man's hand. With her tall slender frame and the slippery curve of her hips and the unusual straightness of her carriage and with her head arched back ever so slightly she appeared rather like a model on a catwalk or rather she would have appeared as such if she were not now engaged in conversation with four men standing raptly but with critical eyes in front of her. It was as if the model had stepped down off the catwalk and into her audience and was now reviewing its predispositions and becoming displeased with what she was discovering.

"I like to be helped on with my coat, but not if it means I should be a passive wimp," she said.

Then a man spoke but I couldn't make out his words. She replied, "Sure I want power. I want the power to control my own life. Which reminds me: I need to get home immediately. Bye."

And with her hips swinging she was out the door. The anthropologist was still detailing to me the sexual practices of his tribe.

****

The following Friday I arrived early at the salon and to begin with stayed in the front room. I chatted with a young married woman looking for sexual adventure, then three surprisingly articulate members of a rock band. Later I became part of a loose group listening to a co-ed's account of being arrested and groped at a civil-rights sit-in. She was describing one of the groping officers when Simon, accompanied by a sullen young man I had not seen before came up to me.

"This is Michael Bowen, the person who organized the Human Be-in."

For some reason I was rendered speechless. Bowen didn't say anything either and stared at me as if he were being shown a mounted fish. I managed a few words but Bowen said nothing, gave nothing and moved on, Simon following. I recalled too late that John Thompson had mentioned an artist named Bowen. Now abandoned and standing self-consciously surrounded by the chattering Berkelyites, I had a flash of nostalgia for Puritan Avenue, when from behind someone tapped me on the shoulder. I turned around. It was her.

"I don't suppose you remember me."

"Oh, but I do."

"How could you? We only glanced at each other in passing and that was . . . "

"Eight weeks ago."

We were both momentarily taken back by the exactness of my instant recall.

"You remembered me; why shouldn't I remember you?" I pleaded.

She smiled but it was the kind of slow, low-lidded smile that people give you when they know something that you don't. I was expecting her to say something, but instead her hazel eyes signalled me to look at her green leather bag resting on her hip. When I did she patted it slowly. It looked old, its embroidered leather cracked, and very expensive.

"Ok, I got it. You secretly captured my alter-ego and now you carry it around in your bag."

She liked that. "You're closer to the truth than you think."

"Can you take me the rest of the way?"

"I was standing where you are now. And you went into that room with Simon and a young man in a suede jacket covered with fringes . . . "

"John Thompson."

"And you left the door open and I stood there and watched."

She stopped.

"And what did you see?

"Well, I don't know what I saw. That's why I'm talking to you now. I couldn't figure it out. On one level it looked mundane: three guys looking at a poster and talking about it. But in that moment when we made eye contact there was something about the expression on your face that made me think something significant was about to happen to you. So I watched you through the doorway and I was right. I couldn't tell what was happening to you, but I could tell from the expression on your face that it was profound. It was almost like your soul was naked."

I had lost my cool now and she saw it. I didn't know what to say. She helped me out.

"Have you guessed yet what's in my bag?" she asked, obviously trying to take the pressure off me.

"No."

She took hold of my hand and placed it on her bag. Its leather was soft and pliable. A biggish object was at the bottom and I squeezed and felt around it

"A camera."

"Bravo."

The memory of several flashes of light as I stood with Simon and John in front of *Flower Child* came back to me.

"You took pictures?"

"And I got one remarkable shot of you."

"Do you always carry a camera around with you?"

"Not in the shower. And usually not when I go to bed."

"Well thank God for that. And so you're a photographer then?"

"That's right."

"Can I see it?" I had regained enough of my cool to think tactically now.

"See what?"

"The remarkable shot."

"Well I don't have it with me. It's at home?"

"Will you take me there to see it?"

"No, I won't." She broke off eye contact and looked at her watch. Then she looked me hard in the eyes.

"I'll go home and get it for you," and now her words came out slowly, "if you will then explain to me what I saw."

"It's a deal."

"Okay, I'll be back in twenty minutes."

****

When she left I looked for Calhoun. He had asked me to speak to him before I left. I found him in the front room. He went off to get something and returned with a thick letter-size manila envelope.

"I'd appreciate it, Mike, if you'd have a look at this stuff. I'm chairman of something called the Committee for Economic Reconversion. The idea is to show people how the economy could be converted to a peacetime economy without causing unemployment. This is some of our stuff. I thought you might be able to offer some suggestions. If not, that's okay."

****

Twenty minutes later my eight-week obsession appeared in the entrance hall. I raced over. She was holding a large manila envelope like the one Calhoun had given me.

"I was afraid you wouldn't come back."

"I generally keep my word."

"I don't know your name."

"Julie."

"That's much better than the one I'd given you."

"Given me?"

"I've thought of you once or twice. So I had to give you a name."

"What?"

"Don't you want to know *my* name?"

"Of course I do."

I was smiling but she wasn't.

"Which do you want first?"

"Mine." I saw a hint of a smile.

"The Green Handbag."

"THE GREEN HANDBAG!"

She frowned. Then smiled. Then quickly added, "And yours?"

"Mike."

"Pleased to meet you, Mike." She took hold of my hand in a mock handshake.

"Ok, now that we've got the name-thing done, I really would like to see the photograph."

She handed me the envelope.

"You may keep it."

I thanked her profusely and then carefully pulled out the biggest photo of myself I had ever seen. It was a black and white, head and shoulders photograph of me looking at the *Flower Child*, the poster starkly visible with my face in front of it and half turned to the doorway. I have never been vain about my looks, but I could not help but be impressed and a little frightened by the intensity of interest that she had captured on my face. Without saying anything I raised my eyes to look at the photographer. She appeared moved by my reaction.

"Ok, now why do you look like that in the photo?"

"Well, I'll try to give it to you straight Julie, but . . ."

"Say it again."

"Say what?"

"My name."

She was very East-Coast and I knew what she was after, so I wrapped up her name in my strongest drawl.

"*Julie.*"

"That's wonderful. No one's ever said it like that before. Where're you from?"

"Nebraska."

"I've never met anyone from Nebraska before. Sorry, I shouldn't have said that."

"It's alright. I'm used to it."

"So you're going to tell it to me *straight*."

"Yes, but I don't know if I can handle questions. And I haven't had dinner yet."

"What's that got to do with it?"

"Maybe we could go someplace and have dinner together."

"I can't. I'm expected home."

"I don't have wheels. Can you give me a lift to The Med?"

"On Telegraph?"

"Yah."

She thought a minute.

"Ok, but we have to go *now*."

And so we did. We stepped out the door and seconds later I was sitting next to her in her newish VW bug. I intended, on the one hand, to keep my word and tell it to her straight, but on the other I didn't really want to explain to her the significance of my encounter with a poster and its creators. Somehow I didn't think she would identify with my story. So when she inserted the key in the ignition and said she had to stop at the post office, I tried to turn our conversation down another road.

"Isn't it closed?"

"They keep it open till late for people like me who have post-boxes there."

"How come you have a post-box?"

"When I moved out here from New York City a few months ago I didn't have a permanent place to live. I haven't checked my box for a couple of weeks."

"What brought you to Berkeley?"

"I needed a new life."

"That sounds dramatic."

"Speaking of drama, are you going to tell me about it?"

I hesitated. "As you can tell, I don't really want to. But I also usually keep my word. I'll tell you when we pull up at the post office."

****

We came to a stop in front of a long neoclassical stone building. Julie turned off the engine and then turned to look at me.

"I'll try to help you," she said. "Are you an artist?" .

"I used to be. But no, I'm an economics graduate student."

"When? I mean when did you use to be an artist?"

"When I was growing up. I gave it up when I turned sixteen."

"Why?"

"My father promised to buy me a car if I gave it up."

"You gave up your art for *a fucking car*?"

"Sure."

"I wouldn't give up my photography for all the money on Wall Street."

I couldn't think of anything to say. She looked furious.

"I'll be back in a minute."

She jumped out and slammed the door. I watched her race up the broad steps. Her reaction to my story was worse than I had expected. My hope – and maybe this was the first time I acknowledged it – of winning her affection now looked lost. Meanwhile a car had pulled up behind and in the rear view mirror I saw two people talking to each other. This reinforced my feeling of rejection. Five minutes passed with my thoughts drifting halfway across the continent.

Julie returned with an assortment of envelopes and laid them between us. Neither of us spoke. Instead of starting her car she just sat there and looked straight ahead. Her silence had a strange effect.   It established intimacy. Almost total strangers don't sit together in silence by choice, but in this case it was hers.

"So you haven't drawn or painted since you were sixteen?" I know that combination of words sounds a bit sarcastic, but there was none of it in her voice.

"No, that's not quite right." She was looking at me now.

"What is right?"

"I painted last night."

I don't think anyone had ever looked at me so intensely as she did now.

"When did you start again?"

"Almost eight weeks ago."

Now a whole minute must have passed without a word being said. For part of it she was looking at me, part of it not.

"What's your last name?"

"Hope."

More silence.

"Is it alright if I call you Michael?"

"Why Michael?"

"I think Michael would be a better name for you. Mike is too short. And Mike Hope sounds like a comedian. You're not a comedian, are you?"

We both laughed and some of the tension blew away.

"Michael Hope would be a better name for an artist, or even for an economist."

"Have you forgiven me then?"

Rather than ask me what I meant, she thought it through.

"If I'd been in your shoes and in Nebraska I might have gone for the car too."

"So then maybe you'll consent to have dinner with me another night."

"I can't. I'd like to, Michael, but I can't."

"Are you married?"

"No, nor do I have a boyfriend."

"Why not then?"

"Because my life is a bit complicated at the moment. Maybe in a few months."

"That's a long time."

"Not nearly as long as you've gone without painting."

I didn't respond.

"We'll probably meet again at Simon's."

"I don't like the probably part."

"Give Simon your phone number and maybe I'll phone you sometime."

"Why Simon?"

"He's turned one of my photos into a poster and I expect there'll be others. So I keep in contact with him."

"*Probably* we'll meet again and *maybe* you'll phone me. Can we make it more definite than that?"

She didn't answer. I waited. Now her eyes were turned away from mine. It was thinking time again.

"Do you know Country Joe and The Fish?" Now she was looking at me.

I had to think for a moment.

"Aren't they a local rock group?"

"They have a song I especially like. It's called 'Who am I?' Twice since we parked here I've thought of its lyrics."

She fell silent.

"Go on."

"The first time was when I was going up the steps to the post office. It was about you that I was thinking and I'm not going to tell you the words. But just now it was about me that some of the lyrics sang in my mind." Again she stopped.

"Tell me."

"You promise not to ask questions."

"I promise."

"Ok. It's just two lines.

There were some things I loved one time,

But the dreams are gone I thought were mine.
The economist in you probably thinks me and those words silly."

"Yah it does, but there's more in me than just that."

"I know."

"Furthermore, speaking of dreams, I have a new one."

"What's that?

"That you'll phone me sometime."

She laughed. "You'll have to wait for the wheels of fate to decide."

"That's sound poetic."

"I am drawing on that song again."

"You a big fan of Country Joe and The Fish?"

"I'm getting to be. They hired me for a photo session recently. That's how I got to know them. But I think they're going to be famous soon. They're about to re-launch. You've never heard them?

"Fraid not."

Julie's final words to me that evening, as I was getting out of her double-parked car, were, "In case you're interested, Country Joe and The Fish have a gig Sunday night at the Jabberwalk."

****

The Med was warm and smoky and half-empty. The Greek kitchen at the rear was closing. The chef, Dimitri, in his whites and tall hat served me his last portion of moussaka and some Greek salad and a slice of baklava for dessert. I paid a dollar-something and carried my tray over to one of the round marble-topped tables near the front and sat down. Med food had never tasted so good. At first all my thoughts, all of them speculative, were about Julie and then about the good taste of the moussaka and about how good it was to be alive and to be eating and to be young and in Berkeley and it was only when I finished eating that I peeked at the photo. I wanted to pull it out and look closely at the image that I only partly recognized. But I didn't want anyone, like the man in a trench-coat now sitting at the next table, to see it. I was thinking of going up to the bar and getting a coffee, but then remembered I could get a glass of wine at Enzo's. It felt like a special night and, even though I was alone, I didn't want to go home yet.

The night walk across the deserted unlit campus was always a bit spooky. Tonight when I heard footsteps coming closer behind me I instinctively walked faster. I was glad to reach the Southside where there were street lights and people on the sidewalks and where Enzo's was warm and slightly busier than The Med. With a glass of Chianti I sat down at a table off to the side where I could watch people coming and going. I had been sitting there ten minutes when the man from The Med in a trench-coat entered. You couldn't help but notice him because clearly he was a man out of his element, not just for Enzo's, but for Berkeley. He was 35-ish, dark-haired, hadn't shaved for a couple of days and looked like he'd be more at home at a race track than in a library. But I was too busy thinking about other things to think about the oddity of his reappearance. I was thinking about the strange day I had planned for the morrow. It meant getting up before dawn, so I left Enzo's just past ten and was in bed before eleven. Against all the odds, I fell straight asleep.

****

It was still dark when the alarm went off and for a few minutes I laid there in the dark recalling the dream I had been having. It was my recurring nightmare except I had not woken up and by the time the alarm went off I had sighted land – not my land of old but a new unknown land.

This was the day I was to do my mother a favour I had been putting off. She wanted me to visit an old friend of hers from Lincoln, Mrs Youngscap, who had moved to California and now lived down the coast in Santa Cruz and was recently widowed. According to my mother she had known me when I was a child and had once given me a Parcheesi Board, but all I could remember about her was her over-sized pointed nose. After months of delay I had contacted her and arranged to go to her house for lunch. Getting there meant walking down University Avenue, further than Calhoun's house, to catch a bus that would drop me off at the Greyhound Bus Station in Oakland. From there I would have a two and a half hour ride to Santa Cruz.

It had not yet gone seven when I left home in the dark. A damp wind was blowing and Berkeley was still asleep. Except for the occasional car, University Avenue, the whole boring two miles, belonged exclusively to me. The tall utility-pole street lights smeared everything, the shop-fronts, the asphalt and even my hands, with urine-colored light. Nothing was open, not even the "All-Night" burger joint.

When I reached San Pablo Avenue it was still dark and still dead. I crossed over San Pablo's four empty lanes to a bus stop. There was no shelter, just a sign on a post next to a street light and lower down on the post a bus schedule. There was just enough of the urine-colored light for me to read it. The bus that would take me to the Greyhound station was due in twenty minutes. Two other people, both apparently on their own, were waiting. One was a young woman whose nurse's uniform showed below her dark jacket. The other was a poorly dressed black man in his fifties. We all avoided eye contact and kept our distance. A quarter of an hour passed and it was beginning to get light and I was seriously bored. I started gazing behind me and up and down the street. About sixty feet away a man in a trench-coat was leaning against a shop front holding his newspaper up and opened wide in front of his face. I instantly realized it was the trench-coat man from last night, the one who had taken the table next to mine at The Med and who then later reappeared at Enzo's. He must be following someone, I thought. But nothing was open and no one was around except the three of us waiting for the bus. I looked at my two companions. The nurse wouldn't have been hanging out last night at The Med and Enzo's, and if the black man had done so I would have noticed him for sure. It was only at this moment that my little mind grasped the obvious: Trenchcoat was following ME. Suddenly I was terrified in a way that I had never been terrified before. How could this be happening? Why would anyone want to follow Mike Hope? There was no reason for this to be happening, but it was, and I think that it was because there was no reason that I was so terrified. Sure, I had been hanging out a bit with artists and activists, people that the folks back home wouldn't approve of, and I had smoked some dope and helped myself to some premarital sex, and committed many felonies in the process, but all that could not explain what was happening to me now. And then I began to think through the logistics of what was happening and I got even more terrified. Here are some of the thoughts that raced through my mind.

"That Trenchcoat bastard must have been watching my place all night. How else could he have followed me down here. But he couldn't have stood out there on the street all night waiting for me to go out in the morning. He must've had a car to sit in. But he must've followed me on foot from The Med to Enzo's. Shit, it must've been him that I heard coming up closer to me in the dark as I walked fast and then faster across the campus. Fucking hell! But to have followed me to The Med would have required a car. My God, are there two of them? When Trenchcoat saw me enter Enzo's he could've used the public pay phone at the corner to contact his partner through a phone answering service or maybe they had walkie-talkies or radios. His partner could've brought the car around to near Enzo's and then at a distance followed Trenchcoat following me on foot. Through the night they could've taken turns sleeping and watching. Yes, there are definitely two of them. Maybe more. But why? How can this be happening? What should I do? Keep cool! Keep cool, Mike! But who are they? Some kind of secret police? Of course. The FBI probably. But why? Why would they, why would anyone want to follow me, Mike Hope? Michael Hope, ha ha. Fuck. And day and night. Watching my fucking door all night long. But what to do? It's really happening. The bastard is there behind me. He'll be looking to see if I've noticed him and connected him with last night. So far I'm in the clear. I turned back around immediately when I recognized him and I've not turned around for a second look. That would be a giveaway. I must keep it like this. At this hour on a Saturday the bus will be nearly empty. I'll take a seat a few rows back on the right-hand side. And I won't allow myself to look out the window at people boarding after me. But I'll be able to sneak a look at Trenchcoat when he's paying his fare. He'll take a seat at least a few rows behind me. When he passes I'll be reading the book I've brought with me."

When the bus arrived there were five of us waiting, not counting Trenchcoat. I was still terrified. I boarded first, took an aisle seat near the front, got out from my little rucksack Raymond Chandler's *The Big Sleep* and watched Trenchcoat pay. I opened my book to a random page and from the corner of my eye glimpsed creamy folds of fabric as Trenchcoat passed.

"Don't look back." I kept telling myself that as the bus passed into Oakland and reached the bus station and I got off, bought a ticket, went straight to the loading platform and joined the short waiting line. A bus was already there but no driver. It was not due to leave for another half hour. I could feel the line growing longer behind me. "Don't look back." Finally the driver arrived, opened the door and started taking tickets. I took a seat in the second row, got out my Chandler and prayed that it had all been just a scary coincidence. But a few minutes later I watched Trenchcoat give his ticket to the driver. I looked down at my book. Again I glimpsed the creamy folds of his coat.

It was the longest bus ride of my life and although at times I pretended to be reading I was not really doing so. I tried to think of a reason why I was being followed, but could think of none. The only thing I could think of was that it had something to do with my visit to Calhoun's salon.

I made sure I was the first off the bus. Despite my defective hip I can, if need be, walk very fast. Exiting the bus station I found myself racing down a long, straight pedestrian way. After two hundred yards I entered a drugstore and asked a customer where the local library was. I left the big drugstore by a main street entrance and five minutes later I took a book off a shelf and then at a table near the back of the reading room took a seat from where I could watch the door. Thirty minutes passed and no Trenchcoat. Of course his partner could have entered, but I had observed no likely suspects.

Could he be waiting for me outside? No, because he must have been following me to see who I was going to meet and the library would be a good place to meet someone, so if they still had my trail one of them would come into the library.

Suddenly I had a thought that almost make me laugh out loud. If I had not discovered that I was being followed, Trenchcoat would have followed me to the house of my mother's friend and then maybe they would have started following her. After all, the fact that I snuck out in the wee hours under the cover of darkness to go meet her was proof that she was a key player in this sinister conspiracy.

From the phone booth in the library's entrance I called a cab. Ten minutes later it pulled up in front and I dashed out and jumped in. I could not resist looking back from time to time to see if we were being followed. We were not.

****

I stood in front of the white frame house and watched my taxi drive away. It was a small house, much older than me, with a red brick chimney, green shutters and a view of the sea. The garden gate clanged shut behind me. A tall clay urn overflowing with scarlet flowers stood next to a shiny black panelled door. Before my finger found the bell the door opened. There stood Mrs. Youngscap with the long pointed nose that I remembered and bangs of silver hair and small dark eyes that seemed to be waiting for me to say something delightful.

"Oh Mrs Youngscap how lovely it is to see you here on this beautiful day high above the sea."

It was true that the sun had come out, but I could hardly believe I had said that. Mrs. Youngscap, tall and straight and wearing a dark blue dress with large white polka-dots, looked delighted. I was no longer sure life was real.

Inside, Mrs Youngscap invited me to "Make yourself at home while I do some things in the kitchen."

I sat down on her red and blue sofa and laid my head back against a white lace doily and looked across at her empty fireplace. On the mantle stood numerous photo-portraits in gold-edged frames. One, a sepia photo and larger than the rest, was a photo of a man in bib overalls attacking a haystack with a pitchfork. Her father perhaps. To my left an enormously fat black cat slept stretched out on a red velvet pillow in front of a big low window overlooking the blue-green sea. Roast chicken smells drifted in from the kitchen. Where was Trenchcoat now I wondered?

Back then I could occasionally be witty and very occasionally interesting but never charming. Yet that afternoon, sitting in Mrs. Youngscap's little parlour sipping her tomato and celery juice cocktails and then dining at her white linen-covered dining table, I think I did charm her. I carved the chicken and we talked about how apples no longer had the flavour they once had, and about how life was so difficult before Saran Wrap, and about the vanishing art of rolling pie crust, and about her favourite TV programs, and about other things of even greater fascination.

****

When I got out of a taxi in front of the bus station I immediately boarded my bus. It was empty. This time I took a seat at the very back. By the time we left only half a dozen people had boarded and I had seen no sign of Trenchcoat or possible associates.

****

As I approached along the side of the house to the exterior door to my apartment I was thinking about the late dinner I was going to cook for myself. Night had fallen and there was no light back there and it was only when I went to put the key in the lock that I realized the door had been jimmied.

I kicked the door open, stuck my hand inside and flicked on the overhead. The room had been turned upside down.

I looked first at the round table between the two basket chairs on which I had left the two large manila envelopes that I had returned with the previous night They were gone. But my alien image in Julie's photo looked up at me from the floor, and the scores of sheets of paper from Calhoun's envelope were scattered about. I soon realized that they accounted for most of the mess on the floor. Most of the drawers in the room were at least partly open, but only two had been dumped

I didn't sleep much that night, despite drinking four glasses of wine and barricading my door with my chest of drawers. I got up late, showered and then phoned my landlord and the police. The latter, when I told them nothing had been stolen, were not interested. The landlord said he would send a locksmith around on Monday. I decided what I now needed most of all was to talk to Calhoun, but I didn't have his number, nor could I remember his last name. I decided to drop in at Enzo's, as

Calhoun sometimes stopped in there on Sunday mornings. On the way I bought a newspaper, and I sat at Enzo's reading it for an hour but Calhoun didn't turn up. Then, just as I was leaving, Alan appeared.

"Hey," he began," I saw you leave with that photographer woman Friday evening. How did you make out?"

"I'll tell you some other time. I'm in a hurry and I need to talk to Calhoun. It's important. What's your phone number?"

I walked back to my place to phone. Calhoun answered. When I started to tell him about my misadventures he interrupted me.

"I think we should meet somewhere to talk about this. I'm tied up this afternoon, but I could meet you at The Forum at say six-thirty. We could eat there."

I agreed. As soon as I put down the phone I realized Calhoun had suspected that one of our phones was tapped. The Forum seemed an odd choice. It was the coffee house one went to when one wanted to be seen.

****

It was a long afternoon. The season of three, four and five day rains had begun, and now it looked like one was moving in. I took an umbrella with me to The Forum. Calhoun, bless him, was already there, standing by the coffee counter in his old tweed jacket and his plaid cap in his hand. It being Sunday evening The Forum was half empty. Like The Med, there was a Greek kitchen toward the back. After we had filled our trays and paid, Calhoun said, "Let's go to the backroom."

"What backroom?"

"Follow me."

Beyond the tables furthermost from the broad glass front we passed into another room, dimly lit with a dozen square marble-topped tables, none of them occupied, and a fireplace in which flamed one of those imitation log gas fires. We took a table near the fireplace.

"I think it unlikely that we'll have eavesdroppers in here," said Calhoun with a wry smile and then his expression changed to dead serious. "Tell me exactly what happened, and then I'll see if I can think of an explanation. Take your time. But before I forget," and his expression changed again, this time to amusement, "I've had a communication about your name."

"What?"

"Apparently Julie, the photographer that you seem to have met Friday evening, talked to Simon yesterday and told him that you now prefer to be called Michael, instead of Mike."

"She said that? I don't believe it."

Calhoun laughed. "I don't exactly know her, but it's clear she isn't your ordinary piece of work. Simon, who seems to have taken a liking to you – and don't worry, I don't mean in his gay way – says he's going to start calling you Michael. But I'll continue to call you Mike if you prefer. Have a think. Now tell me all about it."

So while we ate I told Calhoun more or less what I have told you. He listened intently, nodding his head occasionally. He only interrupted me once and that was to ask for a fuller description of Trenchcoat. By the time I had finished telling my story we had finished eating. Calhoun leaned back in his chair and got out his pipe. I still had not seen him smoke it.

"Mike, Michael . . . ."

""Okay, make it Michael."

"I'm going to tell you a story about myself. It's a story I've never told anyone in full."

"Why tell *me*?"

"Because I feel obliged to tell you. You've had this horrible experience, and it's happened because of your association with me."

"With you? What do you mean?"

"Think about it. We've been seen together one-on-one in public on a fairly regular basis for several months, and now you're coming to my place on Fridays. And then the other night you left with a large envelope."

Calhoun paused, gazed down at his pipe, then looked me straight in the eyes.

"Once or twice in our leisurely conversations at Enzo's I thought I detected in you curiosity about how and why at thirty-something I made the jump from the depths of the Deep South to California. Am I correct?"

"Yes."

"Well, back in the early Fifties, before the Brown versus the Board of Education decision and before Martin Luther King made it marginally acceptable – well at least maybe in the North – I got involved in the Civil Rights Movement. Except back then there wasn't any name for it. And it was the McCarthy Era and I was in New Orleans. That's where I was based all those years I was a seaman. And in between stretches at sea I did a degree in philosophy there at Tulane and then at the end I was a graduate student there."

"The thing we worked at mostly was getting Negroes registered to vote. In the Deep South that was and still is the most subversive thing one can do. Among whites it is considered the ultimate evil. Over half the population in New Orleans was black, but less than five percent of eligible blacks were registered to vote. So we worked quietly and after a few years we got that figure up to 28 percent. And then that figure became public and all hell broke loose. And the worst of it was that the Senate Internal Securities Committee, the Senate's equivalent of HUAC, came to New Orleans to persecute us."

"Its chairman Senator Eastland is from Mississippi where I grew up. More extreme racists have scarcely ever existed. He took his committee around to places as a means of pillorying people working against segregation. The tactics he used were the same as those used by McCarthy in his House Un-American Activities Committee. Everyone subpoenaed to testify he painted as a Communist agent of the Soviet Union. And the method of doing so was always the same."

"As you know the Fifth Amendment says Americans can't be forced to testify against themselves. But the way they interpret it when you're called before a Senate or Congressional Committee it's all or nothing. If you answer one question you're then required to answer every question. If you refuse to answer a question after answering one or more questions, then they say the Fifth no longer applies. So if you then refuse to answer a question they throw you in prison. After a few months they may call you back and ask the same question again. If you then refuse again, they throw you back in prison and so on and so on until you answer or die. What they're after, in addition to making people think you're a Communist and that letting blacks vote is a Soviet plot, are the names of people who have helped you behind the scenes. They are generally well-to-do people in the local community called "angels" who give money to finance anti-racist campaigns, like registering non-whites to vote, but who would lose their job or worse and put their families in danger if it became known they were anti-racist."

"So the Eastlands and McCarthys know that we can't answer all their questions. And therefore they also know that the all-or-nothing interpretation makes it impossible for us to answer any of their questions. And of course that makes it dead easy for them to make it appear that whoever they're interviewing is a Communist. Senator Eastman accused me of being an agent of the Soviet Union. They begin by asking you if you are a member of the Communist Party. But if you're unwilling to disclose the names of the angels, then you can't answer no. So if you also don't want to go to prison you have to say, one way or the other, that you are refusing to answer on the grounds that it may incriminate you, which of course makes it sound like you are a Communist, which of course is what they're after. After they've asked you ten such questions you'll, whoever you are, sound like a hard-core Communist, even if you're only an Eisenhower Republican."

"Anyway that's what happened to me. They had me up there for over an hour. When I left the court house with my head still spinning from the ordeal, two state policemen came up to me and told me it was best if I left Louisiana immediately. They said they'd give me twenty minutes to pack and then follow me to the border. The only choice they gave me was which border. I chose Texas. So I drove home, threw some of my stuff in suitcases and boxes and then headed west. They followed me all the way to the Texas border.[4]"

"And then I just kept driving until I got to the Pacific Ocean. I spent a few months in and around LA, and then got the idea that northern California and Berkeley might suit me better."

"And so here I am."

He fell silent. But I was too dumbfounded to say anything

"So what," he continued, "has all that Deep South shit to do with you being followed in Berkeley? Well, when I was doing the voter registration thing in Louisiana I was aware from time to time that I was being followed, presumably by FBI agents. J Edgar is of course a resolute racist. And when I started working here in the anti-Vietnam War movement I was of course again picked up by their radar. And because I'd previously been picked up in a big way, they must now regard me as a big fish. I presume that they follow me a lot, maybe all the time, and that my phone is tapped. But except in special circumstances, like when you

---

[4] You may read in full Calhoun's testimony to the Senate Internal Securities Committee at
http://archive.org/stream/scopeofsovietact1112unit/scopeofsovieta ct1112unit_djvu.txt

phoned today, I don't pay any attention to them. For a few days last week, however, I was on my guard."

"Why?"

Calhoun didn't answer at first. Telling his story had obviously been painful for him.

"It has to do with the Committee on Economic Reconversion that I told you about. A few months ago one of its members who I don't really know said he'd been told that if you wrote to the Defense Department – he had a special address for it – and asked them for the names of all the current holders in your state of defense contracts, they would send you the list. I said sure, go ahead and try, but I didn't take it seriously."

"Then about a week ago after our weekly meeting he handed me a bound stack of computer printouts thicker than the San Francisco phone book. It consisted merely of the names and addresses of California people and companies and the dollar size of their contracts. What was interesting was that nearly all the contracts – thousands and thousands of them – were for relatively small amounts, like between five and fifty thousand dollars. Clearly this is one way they maintain support for the war. We quickly identified local and state politicians who had these contracts. So we now have a way of discrediting them when they publicly support the war."

"To begin with two of us interviewed a small wholesale grocer on the list. He said a defense department agent had approached him a couple of years ago asking for baked beans. They offered him a price that would give him nearly a hundred per cent profit. So of course he said yes. Now once a year he makes a phone call to a larger wholesaler and has them ship the beans to an army base. For this he clears $11,000. He said he doesn't really support the war but wasn't going to speak out against it or let anyone in his family do so because he would then lose half his income."

"But then I developed misgivings about keeping the list. – I mean me personally keeping it. In Berkeley you have to assume that with any open working group at least one of its members will be an undercover agent of some kind. And they'd soon know of the good use we were going to make of the list."

"So I made a call from a payphone and then after losing any undercover boys following me, I handed over the list to someone not associated directly with our committee. They probably had been waiting for a chance to search our house, but that's not easy because Simon works there all day from the lower level. When Friday night came and they saw you leave with a thick envelope, they must've thought I'd given you the list or at least a large chunk of it. And then when they saw you sneak out of your place when it was still dark they must've thought they were really on to something."

Calhoun laughed. "Were you carrying anything?"

"Yah, a small rucksack with a book and a stack of papers relating to my dissertation. I was planning to get some work done on the long bus rides."

Calhoun laughed again. "It's a good thing you lost the fuckers."

"In general what should I do about being followed?"

"Nothing. Just ignore them. If you start looking behind you, you'll start going out of your mind, and furthermore they'll be convinced that you have something to hide. I never look for them unless I'm going to visit an angel up in the hills or I'm doing something special like handing over that list a few days ago, and then I have special procedures for making sure that I'm on my own."

****

The rain had still not yet arrived when I said goodbye to Calhoun in front of The Forum and thanked him profusely. The Jabberwock, another Berkeley coffee house but with live music, was a further ten minutes' walk down Telegraph.

Country Joe and the Fish were in the middle of a set and all the tables were occupied. I stood against a wall and listened for the lyrics Julie had recited to me. But the set ended without my hearing them. A few people left, and three long-haired co-eds, one verging on the beautiful, let me share their table. They assured me that the Fish had not yet performed "Who Am I?" Then midway through the second set they did. Here are some of the song's lyrics.

> *There were some things that I loved one time,*
> *But the dreams are gone that I thought were mine,*
> *And the hidden tears that once could fall*
> *Now burn inside at the thought of all*
> *The years of waste, the years of cryin'*
> *The passions of a heart so blind;*
> *To think that, but even still*
> *As I stand exposed, the feelings are felt*
> *And I cry into the echo of my loneliness.*

> *Who am I*

To stand and wonder, to wait
While the wheels of fate
Slowly grind my life away.
Who am I?

What a nothing I've made of life
The empty words, the coward's plight
To be pushed and passed from hand to hand
Never daring to speak, never daring to stand.

It had passed ten when the Jabberwock's door closed behind me and the music died and a cold wet wind blew in my face. The rain had come. It being Sunday and now cold and raining, the Avenue was dead. The Med was closing down. Inside a young woman was sweeping and mopping up. The Forum's long covered terrace was deserted and the chairs stacked, but the inside was still brightly lit like a Paris café. Three tables were still occupied. Across the street the bookstores were in darkness. The buskers and Barb vendors were long gone, the head-shop's strobe light was off, the Chinese cafeteria was shut. A cop car cruised slowly by. No one else was out. Crossing the campus my imagination and the sound of the rain on my umbrella kept me company. But tonight I heard no footsteps except my own.

When I came out the other side I saw lights still on down at Enzo's. It was too late to look in and I started up Euclid. A score of people were exiting one of the little cinemas. Instinctively I scanned them for Sue. What an absurd thing to do I immediately realized. Some of the cinema goers were running now because of the rain. No, it was worse than absurd; it was pathetic. She was long gone. It was raining harder now. Nor had Julie turned up at the Jabberwock and some bastards had broken into my pad and those fucking lyrics kept echoing in my mind:

Never daring to speak, never daring to stand.[5]

---

[5] "Who Am I?": https://www.youtube.com/watch?v=xg6KLK07Tlk

Part Three – Julie's Dream

"They are not my kind of person." I remember using that expression when I was an undergrad and then in the beginning when I was at Berkeley. I used it or expressions like it not only in speaking to others but also, and more importantly, in speaking to myself. I used to say "He's not our kind of person," or "She, besides not being a man, is a different kind of person than me." But now in my third year at Berkeley I could no longer use expressions like those because I no longer knew what kind, if any kind of a person I was and the longer time went on the more I thought I was no kind. Sure, you can make yourself identify with some group but then you wake up in the middle of the night and the identification is gone, maybe it's gone even with the person sleeping next to you. So it's a bit frightening, or at least I found it so, to discover that you are a real individual rather than just one of some kind, even if it's a small kind.

Maybe that is why now I sometimes found myself thinking – maybe "wondering" is a better word – about Alan – Calhoun and Simon's housemate. It wasn't Alan's harem itself that made me wonder about him but the fact that without his harem Alan was so not-out-of-the-ordinary and yet with it, he was so obviously not any known kind of a person and for a long time now he must have known that. How, I wondered, did he come to be so singular and how did he cope with it? Then one day as I came in out of the rain and into Enzo's, Alan, sitting alone, spotted me and called me over to his table. He had on a new suit. Not new-new, not by at least twenty years, but new to Alan. Like the suit I had seen him wearing a dozen times, this one was double-breasted and dark blue, but the fabric had a soft midnight sheen and white pencil-thick stripes an inch apart. It was the bank's president's suit, but the effect was somewhat different on Alan. As usual, he was tieless and crumpled and as usual, but without letting up on the word flow, his bedroom eyes scanned every woman coming through the door.

"Where do you buy your clothes, Alan?" He visibly liked the question.

"Except for my socks and underwear I buy all my clothes at the same place. A Goodwill shop over in San Francisco in Pacific Heights. It's there for all the richies who are too lazy to give their clothes away instead of throw them away if they have to go further than the corner. I go over there twice a year and stock up. You like my new suit?"

"It looks very Alanish."

"It cost four dollars."

"Have you always been into clothes and women?" The question got a laugh out of Alan. His suit jacket was unbuttoned and behind his white shirt I could see his paunch shake.

"I never thought much about either until I got drafted and finished boot camp."

"You mean you didn't have girlfriends when you were in college?"

"God no! I would've liked to, but they didn't recognize my existence. When it came to girls I was your total loser."

"So what happened?"

"I went to a cocktail party with my parents and it changed my life."

By now I knew Alan well enough to know that he was going to tell me a story, but not before he was sure that I was dying to hear it. And I knew that I soon would be. Once Alan had engaged you in one of his monological conversations, even if it was mid-morning at Enzo's, there was something so compellingly relaxing in his telling that it made you feel as though you were now both settled with a bottle of vintage red on a velvet couch for the evening.

"How could going to a cocktail party with your parents turn you into a ladies man?"

"My father was a non-commissioned officer in the Army."

He paused.

"So?"

"And I grew up back in the interior of California where no one goes and went to the University of Redlands, a Baptist university. Not quite your Nebraska but still halfway to the moon. The week I graduated I went with my parents to an army cocktail party. I'd been drafted and was due to report in a couple of weeks. This came out in the conversation my parents were having with a major, and then the major asked me where I would like to be stationed when I finished boot camp. Well, I had no idea and I was embarrassed and I said San Francisco which of course was ridiculous. But the major said 'Well, I'll see what I can do.'"

"I forgot about it completely, but then at the end of boot camp you're all in a big hall and a sergeant calls out your name and you go up front and he hands you an envelope and inside are your papers telling what army camp you've been assigned to. Well, I'd been assigned to the Presidio. I couldn't believe it. You know the Presidio in San Francisco?"

"Of course I've heard of it and noticed it on the map. It looks huge. It covers half the top end of the peninsula."

"That's right and it's right next to Pacific Heights and Marina. You should go there sometime Michael. It's one of the most beautiful places anywhere – woods and golf courses and a few nice old buildings and all high up overlooking the Bay and Golden Gate Bridge, and best of all, there are almost no soldiers there. I could hardly believe my luck. As a teenager I had dreamed of living in San Francisco, but never expected to and now I was there in the best part of it and with a soft office job. I didn't have a car, but I could walk off base and straight into Pacific Heights and down into the Marina where all the office girls lived. I'd go down there, always alone, and sit in coffee places and go into smart bars and I always went in my uniform, and that's what did it for me. It was long before the war in Vietnam, and back then army uniforms gave off what Simon calls "good vibes", and young women started approaching me. I didn't have to do anything except stand at a bar looking awkward and they would come up to me and start talking. At first I thought they were having me on, and I wouldn't show interest, but that just made them more interested and before I knew it I'd be going to bed with them."

"So you've been in heaven ever since."

"At first it was heaven, Michael, but for me that ended a long time ago."

A sudden change came over him and he stopped talking and broke off eye contact. He looked sullen and troubled.

"What happened?"

"That's another story. Maybe someday I'll tell you. But now I've got be off."

The day Alan told me this story, it was mid-November 1967 and the national consensus of support for the Vietnam War was breaking up. According to Gallup a majority of Americans still supported the war but that majority was narrowing by the week and the people who in their hearts did not support the war increasingly felt it safe to say so. By now there had been a thousand demos, not yet in Nebraska but nonetheless coast to coast, in big cities and small. And then on November 30th Senator Eugene McCarthy officially entered the race for the Democratic presidential nomination running on an anti-Vietnam-War platform.

Meanwhile in Berkeley, where *The Berkeley Barb*'s circulation had overtaken *The Berkeley Gazette's*, I was dreaming of Julie. Every day I thought of Julie and sometimes also in my sleep at night. She had neither turned up Fridays at Berkeley Way nor phoned me, and Simon, who admitted that he had Julie's phone number, refused to give it to me. At Julie's request he had promised not to.

"But I'll tell you her full name."

"What?"

"Julie Newport."

"Is it spelled like it sounds?"

"Yes, but don't trouble yourself; it's not listed."

And it wasn't. But Simon and I were becoming friends. Twice in November we went together in his VW van to psychedelic dance halls in San Francisco, once to the Fillmore and once to the Avalon. Inside, we went our separate ways and then met up at midnight or later. The second time it had been Quicksilver Messenger Service and Big Brother & the Holding Company at the Fillmore, and Simon had made a friend, a man my age with an Afro. So there were three of us in the van on the ride back to Berkeley. I decided it was a good time to make a fresh plea to Simon to give me Julie's phone number. His new friend took my side and when we got back to Berkeley Simon gave me Julie's number.

The next day was Sunday and I decided to wait until evening to make the big phone call. About three, I was at my easel painting a watercolor and trying to think of things to say to Julie, when my phone rang.

"Hello."

"Simon betrayed me last night, so I decided to call you before you got any big ideas."

There was a hint of irony in Julie's voice.

"Just now, I was trying to think of some of those big ideas but I couldn't think of any. How did you find out."

"Simon rang me to confess and to warn me that you would be in hot pursuit. So I decided to call you first to save you the trouble and tell you that I still am not available for your company. But . . . ."

"But what?"

"But I wish I were."

I didn't know what to say, nor did I know if she really meant that last bit or was just saying it to spare my feelings.

"I do, Michael, really."

"Why can't you?"

"I can't tell you. I wish I could, but I can't. Are you still painting?"

"I had to lay a brush down to pick up the phone."

There was a long silence before she said, "Simon says you are the real thing and the most talented artist he knows. I have to go now Michael". She hung up.

In December I phoned Julie four times. The first time she answered but hung up after saying, "I'm sorry Michael, but I don't want to talk to you." The second time someone else answered. It was a young woman's voice.

"Who's calling?"

"Michael Hope."

"I'm sorry, but Julie doesn't want to talk to you."

"Who are you?"

"I'm Charmaine, Julie's housemate."

"I didn't know she had a housemate."

"From what I understand there's a lot you don't know about Julie."

"Like what?"

"I shouldn't have said that. I've got to go now."

I couldn't think of anything to say and I just held the line in silence. I expected her to hang up but she didn't.

"You still there?"

"Yah," I answered.

"Listen, it isn't because Julie doesn't like you that she won't speak to you. It's not that at all. There are other reasons. That's all I can say."

And she hung up.

****

The third and fourth times I called it was again Charmaine who answered. She recognized my voice immediately and hung up with a quick "Sorry Michael."

****

Over Christmas I spent a week with my mother in San Diego. She was doing fine with her new life and I was happy to see that. We spent Christmas Day with my twin sisters and their twin families. I was just about able to conceal my emergent individuality, so there were no real problems and I enjoyed our long Christmas Day, especially the time with my six nieces and nephews. But underneath my good cheer I felt melancholy. My Julie dreams had come to naught. I was also beginning to wonder why I had them in the first place. After all, my total contact time with Julie added up to only about thirty minutes and not exactly intimate ones. And I still knew nothing about her except that she was a photographer, big deal, and carried her camera around with her in a green leather bag.

I was painting less now, even though my first poster, thanks to Simon, had been published. January trudged by, the days short and dark, the nights long and rainy, and day by day my melancholy deepened. More and more I smothered thoughts of Julie in meaningless equations and sometimes whole days passed without my even thinking of her. Then one Saturday night, after maybe a glass too many, I had been in bed and asleep for over an hour when I awoke with a crazy man's idea. "If I phone Julie now" – ten past two my clock said – "she might answer and I can surprise her with a question."

The phone rang twelve times before someone picked it up.

"Hello." It was Julie.

"Will you meet me for breakfast at The Forum at ten to ten?"

I waited and waited and then waited some more.

"Alright."

I hung up.

I set out walking a few minutes before half-past. I thought the chances of Julie showing were only about fifty per cent, but the morning was full of sunshine and being Sunday almost no one was about as I walked across campus. In Sproul Plaza a Dylan busker was sitting on the edge of Ludwig's Fountain performing for himself and his dog. On the Avenue I passed a young couple pushing a baby carriage and then an old man with a walking cane and then I came to one of the most beautiful sights I had ever seen: Julie sitting all alone on The Forum's deserted terrace.

We carried our trays out to a table on the terrace. My phone call had been spontaneous and if you discount her twenty-second silence I suppose Julie's "Alright" was spontaneous also. But now sitting outdoors opposite each other on that sunny but not yet warm January morning, spontaneity was far away. I had had time to think about what to talk about, and Julie must have had such thoughts of her own, and now, victims of our premeditation, we sat there displaying tension to the other.

Despite this I was elated to be in her presence and I felt she was at least happy to be in mine. I asked if there were any photographers she especially admired.

"Cartier-Bresson."

The name didn't mean anything to me. I asked about him and she seemed to tense up even more. So I changed the subject to Calhoun.

"How did that sweet southern gentleman come to live in Berkeley?" she asked. "Do you know? I asked him once, but he avoided answering."

As soon as she spoke those words we each saw that the other recollected that on the night we met I had asked her that question about her and had received no answer. I like to think that what I did next I would not normally have done. Although Calhoun didn't ask me not to pass it on, it was implicit that he told me his story of how he came to live in Berkeley in confidence. From what I could tell, Calhoun's immoderate modesty had not allowed him to tell even his housemates the whole story. But my conversational situation with Julie was desperate and I felt certain she would like and engage with Calhoun's story and I proceeded to tell it. And I was right. Soon, I had her rapt attention. Even Alan might have been jealous. I was so relieved and so wrapped up in the telling that my attention to Julie's face was not what it should have been. I told her about Calhoun's life as a seaman, his days as a civil rights worker before the Civil Rights Movement had really began, about his testifying before the witch-hunt committee and about his escorted drive out of Louisiana to California and eventually Berkeley. And then I began to tell Julie why Calhoun had come to tell me his story. I told her how I had been followed the morning after she and I had met and we had had our chat in her car in front of the post office. It was when I was describing Trenchcoat that I suddenly noticed that an extraordinary change had come and was still coming over Julie. Her eyes were no longer looking at me, her neck was crimson and now the crimson was rising up through her face and even without the crimson her face looked like the face of someone frightened or acutely ill.

"I'm sorry Michael, but I'm feeling ill and must leave."

And without further words she did.

After a week of trying to reach her on the phone, including one middle of the night call, I decided to give up forever on Julie Newport.

****

February was a bad month for me and the first half of March no better. But in that time I did lots of economics. I submitted another paper and nearly finished the first draft of my dissertation. I still painted evenings, although less than before, and I still chatted with Calhoun at Enzo's. But I stopped psychedelizing with Simon at the Avalon and the Fillmore and, most telling of all, I stopped going to the Berkeley Way salon. With the death of my silly undefinable Julie dream I had lost confidence in Michael Hope. Now I was trying to resurrect my old self. But of course it was a hopeless cause and I felt especially forlorn on the weekends. In Berkeley on any evening, but most of all at the weekend, you could suddenly feel lonely if you found yourself walking alone. With all the young people walking in pairs and small groups up and down every street and most in conversation, you saw and heard and almost smelt human companionship. The third Saturday in March I went to dinner at The Med thinking it would be good for my spirits but instead of raising them it lowered them. I was especially down after the long walk home alone. I entertained some pretentious thoughts about the hard times of my forefathers, put on some Baroque and trudged up to my easel where I started painting a dreary landscape. It had gone eight-thirty when there was a light syncopated knock at the door. I opened it and there stood Simon dressed as a pirate.

"I haven't seen you for ages." As he spoke he removed his black eye patch.

"I know. I've been preoccupied with my studies."

"That's bad for anyone, but especially for an artist. I've come to rescue you. I'm taking you dancing."

There was that ironic twinkle in Simon's eyes and we both laughed.

129

"I'm serious. Both the Jefferson Airplane and The Grateful Dead are performing tonight at the Carousel Ballroom."

"Where's that?"

"It's another San Francisco ballroom. It's bigger than the Avalon and the Fillmore. It's Victorian and its dance floor is huge. You'll love it."

"I'm not in the mood."

"You will be once you're there. And I can't go alone, and it could be the greatest acid rock night ever."

"I don't know."

"I was counting on you, Michael. You know I won't go alone."

I didn't know that but I thought of the favours Simon had already done for me.

"Put on your yellow headband and your Chelsea boots and maybe your paisley shirt and let's go."

The Carousel Ballroom was at the intersection of Market and Van Ness, but we couldn't find a place to park down there and ended up parking a mile away. We had started walking when from behind us, clanking down the middle of the street, came a cable car. As it came along side us and slowed from its top speed of nine-miles-per-hour, Simon and I each grabbed hold of a pole and jumped on. Both sides of the cable car were overflowing with long-haired youths in vivid get-ups clinging to the poles. On the pole next to mine was a teenage girl wearing granny glasses. She smiled and passed me a joint. I had a toke and passed it on to Simon who had a toke and passed it on to a conservative looking lady of fifty on the next pole. She declined to partake but, smiling, passed the joint on to the young man sharing her pole. When the cable car came to Market Street most people, including Simon and me, jumped off.

Simon and I paid our three dollars fifty and passed into a lamp-lit parlour with a long oriental carpet and red-velvet couches occupied mostly by long-haired young men, some in top hats and Edwardian jackets, and young women, some in mini dresses, some in long velvet gowns and lace-up boots and some with day-glow painted faces. From the parlour we passed under an archway into a giant high-ceiling Victorian ballroom and there, finding myself inside the lightshow, I went dancing out into the vast waving sea of dancers with the raunchy funky chords and compulsive rhythms of The Grateful Dead. It was an instantaneous high, and I danced straight through to the end of the long set.

Between sets, standing off the dance floor, I watched recording executives in turtlenecks and jeans gauchely swaggering about, and dealers in silk shirts and bellbottoms nonchalantly servicing customers. When the Jefferson Airplane came on stage I decided to go up in the balcony so I would not be tempted to dance still more, or at least not right away, because my hip had begun to ache,

The Airplane took off with "Plastic Fantastic Lover". San Francisco rock concerts were dance concerts, not stage-show concerts, and although people sometimes crowded around the lip of the stage, like a few were doing now, it was the thousand people doing their free-style dancing inside the light show that was the main event. Down there on the dance floor was of course the best place to be, but up in the balcony, standing at the railing and looking down on all the young fluorescence swirling about in the strobing light was wonderful too. But it was more than just the big sight and the big sound that made it wonderful for me. Up in the balcony, and even more so down there in the light show, I felt more in contact with more of humanity than I had ever felt in the town where I grew up. And now there was a tall blond chick standing next to me giving me friendly looks and down below the Airplane was performing "White Rabbit" and when Grace Slick sang "and if you go chasing rabbits" the blond chick slipped me her joint. I had a couple of tokes and then, just after I had passed back the joint and I was having a big rush, I spotted her. Was it for real or a hallucination? Either way she was down there leaning forward on the stage and looking into her camera aimed at Grace Slick.

What I did for the next ten minutes was pure instinct. I don't think I even for a second thought about what I was going to do next. I said bye to the blond and ran down the stairs and through a hallway and started working my way across the crowded dance floor. "White Rabbit" had ended and the band was between numbers now and that made it easier to thread my way through the crowd. Then the Airplane took off again and as Slick sang the opening lines of "Somebody to Love" I caught sight of the back of Julie's head. I slipped past two Hells Angels and now I was six feet behind Julie, dancing and motioning to the man standing next to her to get her to turn around and look at me. Everyone else up there was already looking at me and they had made a little space for the crazy man to do his thing. Julie turned around. Astonishment engulfed her face. Then she smiled, not a smile of courtesy but one of delight. The people who had made space for me were looking at Julie and a couple of them started dancing and soon they were all dancing and still looking at Julie and at me too and still keeping the space open between her and me. But Julie just stood there holding her camera in one hand close to her heart. Her face said she was in a quandary, and I danced harder and wilder and wilder still and stepped up closer to her. Slick must have noticed the little drama unfolding below her, because now, mic in hand, she leaned out from the stage directly over Julie's head and looking down at Julie sang the first verse again.[6]

> *When the truth is found to be lies*
> *An' all the joy within you dies*
> *Don't you want somebody to love?*
> *Don't you need somebody to love?*
> *Wouldn't you love somebody to love?*
> *You better find somebody to love*

Julie started to dance. Through the deafening music I heard a cheer go up around us. Julie, still holding her camera but now with her arms outstretched, was all smiles and looking me in the eyes and without touching we came up close and then danced back, danced up close again and back, and close and back and close and in the circle around us everyone danced and Slick sang and the guitars wailed and the lights flashed and swirled in a thousand colors. Then the song ended and Julie turned and vanished into the depths of the dance floor.

---

[6] https://www.youtube.com/watch?v=AihWtmn9IOM

****

It had gone three when I got back to my flat and turned on the lights. I brushed my teeth, got out of my clothes and got into bed, but I couldn't sleep. I lay there for two hours and more, no turning and tossing, just lying there on my back telling myself over and over that now I was going to go to sleep. But of course I didn't. Going to sleep never works that way and at five-something I said to myself, oh fuck it, and I turned on a light and got out of bed and dressed and decided, what the hell, I'm going to go for a walk.

As you know, the last time I'd left in the dark in the wee hours on a walk I was followed. This time I made sure no Trenchcoat was about. I'd not gone more than fifty yards and already I was feeling good about taking this crazy walk. My hip hurt a little from all that dancing but nothing compared to the good feeling of moving all alone through the night. I headed for the campus, not for the entrance opposite Euclid that I usually entered by, but a little used entrance further down the slope. Even in the daytime there was something magical about entering the campus this way. You soon came into a grove of redwoods, not giant redwoods, but taller than any trees in Nebraska.

And now I was in the grove. It was not yet dawn, still almost pitch dark, and I walked slowly and carefully. Except now and then when I came under dim gleams of moonlight, I couldn't see the trees, but I could smell them and above me I could hear them whispering in the wind.

I came to the gurgling North Fork of Strawberry Creek and then a footbridge and started to cross. In the middle I stopped and leaned over the timber railing, smelling the world, pungent and damp, and listening to the gurgling of the water harmonizing with the tree tops above.

I left the footbridge and the redwoods and headed south toward where the two forks of Strawberry Creek meet. There is a large grove of eucalyptus trees there and they say it is the tallest grove of hardwoods in North America. There was no undergrowth and I walked into the middle of the grove and stopped. Darkness still reigned where I was standing, but now when I looked straight up I could see the faint first light of a new day. To the objective observer I could have appeared deranged because I stood there transfixed with my head tilted back watching in the far distance the day beginning to be. I started to make wishes, wishes for myself of course, but also for all the people I could think of who had helped bring me here to the beginning of this day. I wished first of all that Calhoun would go on being just like he was, and I wished that Alan would find whatever woman or women he was looking for, and that Simon would find the good partner that he deserved. I was wishing John Thompson a whole long lifetime of drawing when I remembered Vanessa and wished that she was now well on her way to becoming an architect. Then I remembered Sue Ruccio and wished that she would find a way through her troubled past and that she was helping others with theirs. I even remembered Mrs Youngscap and wished her more visitors, and then Grace Slick popped into mind and I wished her a long career and somebody to love, and for those people on the dance floor who I would never know and who had not known me but who had made room for me to do my dance and had smiled and danced Julie into dancing too I wished a thousand happy nights. But I didn't know what to wish for Julie, except that she would find her way past her secret difficulties, but then that was really a wish for me too, so maybe in the end all my wishes were selfish, but back then as the grey above the tree tops turned to lavender and the birds began to sing I did not think so nor do I think so now a half-century later, here in a faraway land.

****

Three nights later at half-ten I had just come home when the phone rang. It was Simon.

"I've been trying to get hold of you for the past ten hours," he began.

I explained that I had been in the library all afternoon, followed by dinner and math-tutoring with fellow grad students.

"What's up?"

"I'm picking you up in exactly ninety minutes."

"Picking me up? At midnight on a Tuesday? Are you crazy?"

"Of course I'm crazy, Michael. But I'm picking you up all the same. It's a photo shoot for the cover of *The Saturday Evening Post*. They're doing a big article on the San Francisco poster scene. Gene Anthony is the photographer. You may have met him over here on Fridays. I promised him I would have all my artists there for the shoot."

"Why is he shooting at such an unsociable hour?"

"Because it's taking place at San Francisco's cable car barn, and the cable cars run till midnight. The shoot is scheduled for one. Now get out of your kakis, Michael, and put on your brightest clothes."

I was waiting in front of my house as Simon pulled up in his VW van. As I got in he scanned me with a flashlight and broke into laughter.

"Where the hell did you get those pants? Even I wouldn't wear those. They're fantastic!"

In a dark street near the bottom of Russian Hill Simon parked his van. A few minutes later we walked through a gate into the end of a long brick-paved yard. At the far end a crowd of people were milling about under bright lights. Behind the crowd was what looked like a vaulted brick entrance to the cable car barn. Most of the people were flamboyantly dressed and the light was so bright that as we came up close to the people they looked more flamboyantly real than if it were broad daylight. A lone cable car festooned with yellow and blue flowers stood on a turntable in front of the barn. Simon and I approached the cable car and the flowers from the side. Behind the cable car rose a blank brick wall several storeys high covered with psychedelic posters vibrating in the brilliant light. Facing this at the top of a tall stepladder was a ginger-bearded man fiddling with a camera mounted on a tripod. I was struggling with the idea that I was a part of this scene when from behind me someone slipped their fur-covered arm under mine.

"I told Simon that if he didn't deliver you here I would never speak to him again."

137

Those were Julie's opening words. I can't remember mine, but maybe a minute later I recall asking, "Is this a real mink coat I'm looking at?"

"Yes, it was my mother's. Do you like it?"

"Yes. I especially like the way it feels on my hands and the way it ends at your hips." Julie was wearing a mini skirt.

The artists were out-numbered by non-artists: producers, distributors, printers and the non-artists' wives. When the photographer up on the stepladder told us to mount the cable car or stand beside it there was a stampede led by the wives. Julie and I found ourselves near the back of the group standing in front of the cable car. When the pushing and shoving stopped, Julie slipped out of her mink.

"Here, put it on. Your lovely pants will be blocked from view, but with this you'll be the only man or woman on the cover wearing mink." Amused, she smiled radiantly.

"How can I resist?"

I draped it over my shoulders.

"Turn the collar up."

I did.

"Magnificent!"

She turned around to face the camera and leaned back against me and leaned her head back so that her lovely hair brushed my face. Reaching behind with both hands, she took hold of mine.

There was no need to tell Simon that I would not be riding back to Berkeley with him. Julie's baby blue bug was parked nearby beneath a street light.

"You want to drive?" she asked.

"I don't know. I've never driven in California."

"Well it's about time you did."

The Chevy my father bought me for my sixteenth was a manual, but the bug's four-speed floor shift was new to me. I was relieved when I got us up onto the skyway and then onto the noisy lower deck of the Bay Bridge, and now I had the confidence to ask a big question.

"Why did you leave New York for Berkeley?"

"Everybody asks me that question and I have a lovely answer I always give but I don't want to give it to you because it's a lie. I'm not yet ready to give you the true answer. Maybe I will be in the morning if you're still around."

She placed a hand on my thigh.

"Around where?"

"My bedroom, of course."

She removed her hand and fiddled with a small contraption mounted on the dashboard.

"What's that?"

"A tape-deck."

"I've seen them advertised but . . . "

"This is your big night: your first photo shoot, your first time in mink, your first time driving in California and now your first tape-deck."

I turned my head to look at her.

"Is it okay if I tease you a bit sometimes?" she asked.

"Sure."

"Good. Now I'm going to turn it on very loud."

She clicked a button and returned her hand to my thigh. It was the Doors' "Light My Fire", the eight-minute version.

Julie lived in a posh new apartment building on the El Cerrito side of Berkeley. In the entry lobby next to the locked elevator was a shiny brass panel with buttons and speakers for each apartment and high above it a TV camera.

As we got off the elevator on the third floor, Julie said, "When we go in be very quiet, because Charmaine is asleep."

"Charmaine?"

"My apartment mate. You spoke to her on the telephone, remember? And told you that I wasn't avoiding you because I didn't like you."

"I'm beginning to believe her."

Inside, Julie slipped out of her mink, dropped it on a long white sofa, took hold of my hand and led me down a dimly lit hall. At the end in front of an open door she stopped and faced me holding an index finger in front of her mouth.

We tip-toed into the room. In the faint light I could see two single beds. Julie led me to the bed against the far wall. In it a small child was sound asleep.

"This is my Julie-two," she whispered in my ear, "and in the bed over there is Charmaine's daughter."

"How old?"

"They're both four."

It was after we made love and we were sitting up in bed in her room lit by a warm green light that I got the first instalment of Julie's life story.

"Maybe you should go now, Michael, because I always sleep with that light on."

That light, the only one burning, was a bedside lamp with a pale shade lit with a green lightbulb. Of course I wasn't about to take seriously her suggestion that I might like to leave, but it provoked new thoughts. What was she afraid of and afraid of every night?

I had already noticed that when speaking to me she had a way of closely watching my face that I was unaccustomed to. And now she must have read my mind, because before I could reply she said, "Will you still like me even if I'm not the fearless woman that you maybe thought I was?"

"Of course, and anyway it's already more than just "like".

"What is it then?" she asked playfully.

"I can't think of the word for it just now."

"Well, if you remember it, let me know. In the meantime do you want to know a little bit about my past?"

"I'm dying to know."

"It's not quite your average normal."

"I figured as much."

"Both my parents were Broadway actors." Rather than continue, she just gazed at me.

"That's a good start. Were? You say 'were'".

"My mother died when I was twelve and my father when I was fifteen." Again she fell silent.

"Tell me about your mother first."

"She came from a very rich and very snobbish Boston family. A Social Register family, if you know what that is. She was raised to marry into another rich and snobby family and to be a good wife. But my mother turned out bad."

"You mean good"

Julie now sat up very straight on the bed and this is the story she told me. ------------------------

Yes and she passed on her good-bad to me, and my dream is to pass it on to Julie-two. It began the summer my mother was eleven. She went with her family to New York for a week and stayed in the Waldorf Astoria. One evening my grandmother took my mother to the theatre, a Broadway theatre. I don't know what play they saw, but it made an enormous impression on my mother. In fact it made such an impression that from that day on my mother's dream was to become a stage actress. But of course it wasn't legitimate for a daughter in her family to become an actress, so they treated it as a child's dream that would shrivel and die as she grew up.

But it didn't die. As the years passed my mother learned not to talk about it in front of her parents. When my mother turned eighteen it was time to bring her out as a debutante and her parents scheduled her for a ball. But the night before her debut she ran away to New York to try to make her dream come true.

I'm not sure how long she was there that first time. Maybe only a few weeks. The family sent down detectives to find her and of course they did. They pretended they'd come to help her achieve her dream and then hauled her back to Massachusetts and locked her up in a private asylum in the mountains.

They kept her there for three months. They only let her out when she convinced her parents that she'd come out as a debutante and make herself available for a suitable marriage. But she was already an actress in the making. She waited three weeks and then ran away to New York again. This time she assumed another name and for a while disguised herself as a nun. I don't know how she supported herself. I was only twelve when she told me all this just before she died. But I know she went to acting school for two years and got her first bit part when she was twenty-two. She was twenty-five when she got her first lead. After that she was never out of work.

When my mother was thirty-two she had me and then my sister two years later. When she was forty-four she had a brain haemorrhage in her dressing room after a matinee and died the next morning.

So that was my mother's life. Short but very nice.

My father's life was similar in some ways. But his upbringing could hardly have been more different. He was the son of a school teacher in Indiana and went to university out there. But like my mother he dreamed of becoming an actor and when he finished college he went to New York to give it a go. He too went to acting school, but he didn't start to get much acting work until he was in his thirties. Meanwhile he had survived with odd jobs, mostly in bars. And then one day he met my mother at an audition and a few months later they got married. As it turned out that was a bigger event in my father's life than it was in my mother's. Up to then my father had had a bit of a drinking problem. But with my mother, and soon also with me and my sister, that went away and his stage career took off in a really big way.

When I was five – by this time both my parents were Broadway stars and making lots of money – we moved into a brownstone on the Upper East Side near Central Park. And about a year later they bought an old farmhouse in Connecticut. It was a big house with big porches and big rooms and they fixed it up and filled it with antiques. When my parents were between plays we lived out there on weekends and during school vacations, and my parents' theatre friends also came out a lot to stay. So although we were out in the country there were often lots of people around. And my mother especially liked to spend time out there because the thing she liked doing most, after acting, was photography, and she had a darkroom out there.

When my mother died everything changed. My father started drinking again. At first just a lot and then really a lot. Sometimes I'd find him drunk when I got home from school. And it got worse and within a year his stage career crashed, and he gave up our brownstone – I was never sure if they'd owned or rented it – and he and my sister and I moved out to the farmhouse in Connecticut.

Now every morning my sister and I had to walk down to the highway and wait for the school bus. Our schoolmates made fun of us because not only did we talk funny but also, not having anyone to look after us, we didn't always look respectable. I was only thirteen. With a little help from my little sister, I did all the cooking and cleaning and clothes washing, and as you can imagine I wasn't very good at it. And every night Dad would go out and come back drunk. Roaring drunk. Often it would be the middle of the night and he could be very scary. Really scary. So my sister and I slept in the same bedroom, the bedroom that had a bolt on the door. And that is when I started sleeping with a light on.

When I was fifteen Dad died of kidney failure. His mother was dead and his father was in a nursing home. And my mother had been disowned and disinherited by her family for becoming an actress instead of a debutante. But my aunt, my mother's older sister, let my sister come and live with her family in Boston. But not me. I was sent away to a private boarding school in upstate New York and only allowed to go to my aunt's mansion and be with my sister at Christmas and Easter and for one month in the summer. I mostly hated the boarding school but some of the teachers were very good to me and I've always been grateful for that. And I got on well enough with the other rich girls and I stuck it out until I graduated. When I did, my aunt offered to bring me out at a debutante ball. That was kind of her, really, but like my mother I didn't want any part of that scene. So with $200 I ran off to New York and Greenwich Village. ----------------- --------

At that point in Julie's narrative, Julie-two, wearing pink pyjamas, appeared in the room. She had had a bad dream and was crying. Julie comforted her and then carried her back to her bed. A few minutes later Julie returned, still in the nude.

"Where was I?"

"You had just arrived in Greenwich Village."

"Yes, and I was very lucky. The second day there I found a job at a pizza-joint and a place to sleep. Then I got a job at a Village café, first at Café Wha and then at Café Figaro. Have you heard of them?"

"No."

"That's okay," she said smiling. "I forgot that until I met you, you were Mike Hope."

"Mike Hope will always be a proud part of Michael Hope."

"Well said." She put her arms around my neck and kissed me.

"Getting back to New York," she continued, "you like The Med so you're bound to like the Figaro. Maybe we'll go there together someday."

"That's sounds good, but now I want to get back to Berkeley and to Julie in her bed."

Julie agreed.

It felt very late when I woke the next morning. Julie's side of the bed was empty. I reached over and picked up my watch on the bedside table. Ten fifty-five. I was debating whether to get up or not when Julie, her long auburn hair draped over the white velour of her robe, entered carrying a mug of coffee.

"Drink this and I'll bring you breakfast."

A few minutes later she returned with a tray bearing two plates of toast and scrambled eggs.

"I've never brought a man breakfast in bed before."

"Then why me?"

"Because I think you might reciprocate sometime. That is if you're not frightened away by what I am about to tell you."

"It sounds scary."

"It is."

"I'm not a total coward."

"I know, but you may not be a hero either."

"Oh I'm definitely not a hero type."

"I'm going to tell you anyway, Michael. I decided after our dance together. It's about you being followed all the way to Santa Cruz."

"How can you know anything about that?"

"The explanation Calhoun gave you is a hundred percent plausible, but it's not the real one."

She paused.

"Go ahead, tell me."

"The true story of Trenchcoat starts in New York, in Central Park. But really it began a long time ago when I was nine or ten and my mother was still alive and I started playing with a camera that she no longer used. As I told you last night she was a keen and a very good amateur photographer. What she photographed mostly were her and my father's theatre friends. She would get them to pose for her backstage and on stage at rehearsals and in Broadway bars and restaurants and sometimes at our country house when they came for the weekend. So just as later I imitated my mother by going to acting school, when I was about ten I started imitating her by photographing her theatre friends. But of course usually they wouldn't pose for little me. So I had to shoot them candidly and it was more fun that way anyway. And I got good at it and, without knowing it, developed a style, and my good mother encouraged me. Together we would sit on a couch and review the contact sheets. She would only have prints made of my best shots. That way my mother taught me from an early age to be self-critical. And strangely that's how I got to be a success as a photographer of folk and rock stars. I mean the candid bit. Posed photos didn't fit their rebellious image. And most professional photographers didn't know how to cope with that – they didn't even know how to begin. But I did, and already in '63 I was shooting in and around the folk clubs in the Village for the fun of it and sometimes I showed people the results and the word began to get out and around. And then suddenly I was in demand. Big names and their agents started looking me up and offering me money. I loved acting but never so much as I loved photography, so I quit acting school and became a professional photographer."

"But because I loved it so much, I kept shooting for pleasure, shooting people in the streets and in Central Park and soon I had my first one-woman show in a Village gallery. I was headed for big-time success, and then one day it blew up in my face."

"What happened?"

"It was early morning, the time kids go to school. I was in Central Park near the zoo and I spotted this man standing half in and half out of the bushes about fifty yards away. Instinctively I raised my camera – like I did with you when you were going into that room with Simon and Thompson. I adjusted my telescopic lens and started shooting. I'd snapped about a dozen when to my left I heard a man shout. Then the man I was photographing turned to look and then turned again to look at me. At that point I turned to my right and saw a third man running toward me. He was about fifty yards away, and instantly I turned and ran for the park exit. I made it out and then ran all the way to the nearest subway station. When I reached it I looked back and I couldn't see anyone running toward me."

"Usually I sent my film out to be developed and to have contact sheets printed. This time I did it myself and blew up a couple of prints. They not only revealed what had been going on in the bushes and why I had been pursued, but worse, much worse, I recognized the man. He's famous, not in a showbiz way but in a big big big big money way. Mr. Ultrarich I'll call him. They say someday he might become President."

"Who?"

"I'm not going to tell you, Michael. Not now, not ever. It would put your life in danger, just as mine is now."

My spine shivered.

"For two days I thought I was in the clear. But I didn't know what to do with the photos. And I had no one close to me then, so I had no one to talk to about it. Then one night when I came home from a photo shoot I found my apartment turned over. They had found the prints and the contact sheet, but not the negatives. I was scared shitless and ran off to spend the night with Charmaine. We had only just met but like with you I instinctively trusted her. When I returned to my place the next morning my phone was ringing. I picked it up. 'How much do you want?' a man's voice said."

"I slammed down the receiver. Suddenly I felt very scared, and not just for myself but also for Julie-two."

When Julie was telling me this I wanted to ask her why she didn't just give or even sell the negatives to Mr Ultrarich and have been done with it. But I already knew her well enough to realize that she wouldn't take kindly to this question and so I didn't ask it – or at least not then.

150

That was not the last time that Mr Ultrarich's men phoned Julie, nor the last time they turned over her place. Increasingly terrified she went to a lawyer for advice and came away more frightened than ever. It was the lawyer who suggested she pull up stakes and quietly relocate somewhere else, and when a few days later she realized she was being followed she decided to take his advice. By now Charmaine had become a close friend. She didn't have much going for her in New York and like Julie she had no support. So she agreed to quietly relocate with Julie, and one day flew out to San Francisco with both their daughters. The next day Julie sneaked onto a train to Philadelphia and from there flew to San Francisco. There she heard the schools were especially good in Berkeley and because Berkeley seemed more remote than San Francisco to a New Yorker she crossed the bay and rented the flat in the high security building.

"Of course when I started meeting people here, the first thing they asked is why I'd left New York. So I had to make up a story. I told them that I had decided Manhattan was no place to bring up children, which is not at all what I think, having been mostly happily brought up there myself. I told them I had decided on Berkeley because I had heard it had wonderful schools. At least that was partly true. But my biggest lie of all was I told them my grandmother lived in El Cerrito. You were the first person I didn't lie to when you asked that question. You remember? You asked me 'What brought you to Berkeley?'"

"Yes, and you answered 'I needed a new life.'"

"And that was the truth and that is the reason I had to avoid you."

"I don't get it."

"I couldn't see you, Michael, because right from that first night when we met at the salon, right from our first words together when I made you feel and guess what was in my bag, I felt I couldn't lie to you. So when you would ask me, as you were sure to do, why I had moved from New York to Berkeley and why I needed a new life I would've had to tell you the story I told you just now, not the story I was telling everyone else. But I wasn't yet ready to tell the true story, not even to you. And anyway I thought that if I told you the true story it would scare you away. That was before I knew what a persistent and stubborn fellow you are."

"I'm not really. It was just you."

"Me?"

"My instantaneous, persistent and stubborn attraction for you."

She laughed. "That's nice flattery, Michael, but that's not what I'm looking for."

"It wasn't intended that way."

"I'm teasing, well mostly anyway."

"I know, but why was it that when you finally came to meet me for breakfast at The Forum you suddenly left and afterwards refused to talk to me?"

We were both facing each other, sitting Buddha-like on the bed. She took hold of my hand.

"Because when you described the man you called Trenchcoat I recognized him as someone I had seen at least twice close to this apartment building. Up until then I had thought that Julie-two and I were safe. Suddenly I knew we weren't. Naturally I was terrified. And since then I have seen Trenchcoat numerous times."

"But why did he and his associates follow *me*?"

"That's easy. They saw me leave Berkeley Way, drive home and then, carrying an envelope, immediately return and then immediately leave again, but this time with you carrying the envelope. Then they followed us to the post office. And that must have been the real clincher for them, because the only reason I could've been going into the post office at that hour was to collect mail from a mail box, and then they saw me come out carrying some envelopes. And then we sat in the car and talked for several minutes. They must've already been thinking that I had maybe gone back to my place to get the photos to give to you, and now they were probably thinking that maybe I had been keeping the negatives in the post office box for safekeeping and was now giving then to you. Of course they didn't know for sure, but they couldn't take the chance that I had given them to you either to release or for safekeeping."

"What did the photos show? You haven't told me."

"And I'm not going to tell you because that's not the point. Maybe the police wouldn't want to deal with the photos, but the media would pay big money for them."

"Then why not sell them to the media and be done with it?"

"For two reasons. If I do, it is highly likely that Mr Ultrarich will buy his revenge. He can wait his time and then have his agents or his agents' agents put out a contract to do whatever he thinks would hurt me most, maybe my death, maybe Julie-two's, maybe something else. So that's one reason. But there's another reason, Michael. It would be against my principles. I don't go around photographing people so as to screw up their lives.

I'm not a fucking paparazzi. I'm an artist who uses a camera. And being an artist and the tradition that that entails means an awful lot to me."

"Then why not either just give Mr Ultrarich the negatives or sell them to him?"

"Fuck, Michael. Don't you see, that would be even worse."

"Why?"

"Well for one it would be anti-American."

"Anti-American? That's crazy!"

"Listen, Michael, maybe you're about to get a Ph.D., but maybe you don't know as much as you should about your country. Why do you think people came here and set it up? They came to be free from those places where big money and heredity ruled, where people like you and me could and would be disposed of if we didn't go along with the wishes of a tiny few, and where most people were conditioned or too afraid not to go along with them. Most of history has been like that. But people came to this land with a dream to create a new history, a dream to be free of the tyranny of the very rich. If I let this man buy me when I didn't want to be bought I'd be betraying that dream. And if lots of people started doing that, then in fifty years the President and all the Senators and Congressmen will be owned not by us the people, as in a real democracy, but by all the Mr Ultrarichs, and the day will come when people will truthfully say America is no longer American. But I want America to stay American. That is my dream Michael, and I will fight for it. If necessary I'd even give my life for it."

No one had ever talked to me like that before, and I didn't even begin to know what to think about what Julie had just said or what to say about it, so I tried to get our talk back on a more practical level.

"So what are you going to do?"

"I'm going to stick to my principles. Other than that, I don't know."

We were still sitting face-to-face and Buddha-like and now she leaned forward and threw her arms around my shoulders and looked me close in the eyes.

"Have I frightened you, Michael?"

"A little."

"More than a little, I think."

"Maybe so."

"I'm sorry Michael, but that's the way it is."

"I know."

"Do you want to say goodbye?"

"Goodbye! God no!"

Julie's eyes were still close to mine. Very slowly a smile began to appear in them and I waited for a surprise.

"Then will you be my old man?"

"Old man? What does that mean?"

"It's Greenwich Village talk. It means do you want to sleep with me every night."

Part IV – Martin and Bobbie's Dream

From that morning when I agreed to become Julie's old man I never again slept at my place on Cedar Avenue. In the beginning I didn't spend as much time at Julie's as I wanted because she wanted to integrate me gradually into her daughter's life. I was curious to know who the father was, but it seemed too soon to ask. Julie never mentioned him, not even when it would have been natural to mention him.

Julie worried that if right away I started spending lots of my not-in-bed time in their flat and moved in my books and easel that Julie-two would feel that her life or at least her life with her mother was under threat. Julie wanted to make the changes gradually. So, except at the weekends, I got up early and crept out of the flat without breakfast, even without coffee. But it was too far to walk every day from Julie's flat to my side of Berkeley and then back again in the evening, so within three days of my becoming Julie's old man I bought myself an old banger.

Some mornings on my way back to my place I would stop in at Enzo's for coffee and a croissant. It was on one of those early Enzo mornings that Alan told me the big secret of his life. I was sitting out on the terrace and it was empty except for my table and two others, and across the street the morning sunshine was glimmering on the tops of the redwoods. I was thinking about Julie and Julie-two and I'd finished my coffee and croissant and was about to leave when Alan, coming up off the sidewalk in his banker's pinstripes, stepped onto the terrace, spotted me and came straight over to my table and sat down.

"I was hoping to run into you, Michael. I need to talk to you."

I hadn't seen Alan for several weeks.

"Sure. What about?"

"About how you do it?"

"Do what?"

"Get a relationship going with an older woman?"

"An older woman?"

"Yes, like your Julie."

"From whom do you know about me and Julie?"

"Simon and Calhoun, of course. I've chatted with her a couple of times on Fridays. She must be twenty-four or twenty-five."

"Yes, maybe even twenty-six. Julie is a year or two older than me, Alan; she's absolutely ancient."

"Listen Michael, I'm not talking about old-old. It's just that I'm sick to death of sleeping with twenty-one year-olds. More than anything, more even than getting my architecture degree, I would like to have a permanent relationship and with a woman more my age, and from what Simon and

Calhoun say you may have achieved that and I thought maybe you could give me some pointers as to how to do the same. Every month that goes by I feel more and more desperate."

For some months I had wanted to ask Alan a question, but hadn't dared because it would have been too intrusive and maybe unkind. But now that he had voluntarily exposed his private self and because my question was now so relevant I couldn't resist asking it.

"Alan, have you ever been in love?"

It was immediately apparent from the expression on his face that I had asked the ultimate question. I waited for him to think it over.

"Yes I have. Once long ago. Do you want me to tell you the story?"

"I would like that a lot."

"I've never told it before because it's so absurd and maybe even pathetic. But I've already told you the part that leads up to it and that puts it in context; I mean finding myself stationed in San Francisco at the Presidio and in uniform and suddenly, for reasons I've never quite understood, attractive to women. You remember?

"Of course I do. It's a good story."

"Well the story gets better. The office job I had there at the Presidio was assigning draftees to army bases all over the world. I soon realized that I could assign myself virtually anywhere I fancied, and I started exploring the possibilities. I had just about decided on Tokyo when an office job opening came up at NATO headquarters. In those days NATO headquarters were just outside of Paris. Paris! I could hardly believe it. But there it was on my desk for the taking. So after four months in San Francisco I headed for France."

"When I got there I found that NATO worked only a four-day week, Monday through Thursday. And in those days the exchange rate for the dollar was fantastic. So I teamed together with two of my workmates and rented a flat in Paris in the Latin Quarter. We would get off work at five on Thursday, hop on a train and stay in Paris until Sunday evening, or, if I had something really good going, until early Monday morning."

"As soon as we got into Paris on Thursday evenings we'd go straight to the big cafés at the bottom of the Boulevard Saint Michel and look for tourist girls, usually from the States, to pick up and show gay Paree and eventually more often than not our flat. When the big event happened I'd been living this life for about a year. It was a beautiful summer's evening. It was Thursday and I and one of my flatmates were sitting outside one of the big sidewalk cafes looking for girls. Some Scottish buskers in kilts and with bagpipes were performing in front of us. Then they moved on and I looked to my left and was surprised and delighted to see that the table next to ours was now occupied by two girls. It was at this point that the most amazing thing in my whole life happened. I made eye contact with one of the girls and instantly I felt like I'd never felt before. Later that weekend she and I talked about it and it had been the same way with her."

"Anyway, me and my buddy soon moved over to the girls' table. They were Smith girls, you know from that posh girls' college in the East. They and a third Smith girl were touring Europe for a month and they had saved Paris for the last. The third girl had a bad case of the runs and was confined to their hotel room and I never did meet her. Sarah, that's the name of the one I'd fallen in love with, Sarah and I spent the next eighty-four hours together."

"Those hours were and remain the best hours in my life. None before or since even begin to compare. But then Monday morning came and they were flying back to the States on Wednesday. Sarah and I promised we'd keep in touch and then get together in a year when I got my discharge. Well, we kept in touch for a while but gradually it tapered off. I think she met someone else. Eventually communication stopped. I never saw or heard from her again."

"Well, in time of course I got over it. But what I've never got over – and it's been twelve years now – is the thrill of being with someone you really love. So for twelve years now everywhere I go, I'm hoping that when I look to my left or to my right or across the room I'll make eye contact with a woman that turns me inside out like on that summer evening down on the Boul Mich."

But Alan had decided it was time to give up on finding another love-at-first-sight and thought maybe I could give him some advice on how to build a relationship with a woman whom he didn't love instantaneously. But I couldn't think of any.

"What about you and Julie?"

"That was a sort of first-sight thing too. It was only circumstances that kept us apart for five months."

"Shit. I was hoping you could help me." Alan was clearly disturbed.

AMERICAN DREAMS

****

Of Berkeley's three big cafés, or coffee houses as we called them, I liked The Med the most because there were always people there who were serious about more than just themselves. But although it had a mezzanine, it did not have a terrace, just a couple of tables out on the sidewalk, and what I liked most of all was sitting out in the open air with all the people walking by. So if I wasn't looking to eat and it wasn't cold and rainy, and it was never either cold *or* rainy from April to October, then I usually went to Enzo's or The Forum. But on this night fifty years ago it was April Fools' Day and Julie and I were sitting at that window table in the Caffé Mediterraneum that Dustin Hoffman sits at in *The Graduate*. That filming at The Med had recently taken place but all the really big events of '68, films aside, were yet to happen.

Ignoring the two massacres, Orangeburg and My Lai, the first three months of '68 were an unprecedentedly auspicious beginning for the likes of Julie and me. Week after week we witnessed events that seemed to foretell the end of one era and the beginning of a new one. The first such event dropped into my mailbox the first weekend in January. It was what became known as *Time*'s anti-Johnson issue, its cover bearing a cartoon image of President Johnson worthy of *Charlie Hebdo* and its inside conveying the general message that the President of the United States was a bloodthirsty loser. At the end of February the CBS Evening News anchor Walter Cronkite, or Mr. Middle America as he was known, declared that America's war in Vietnam was a lost cause and in more senses than one. Two days later Secretary of Defence Robert McNamara publicly resigned in tears and in protest against the "Goddamned Air Force" and its recent and still ongoing "Goddamned bombing campaign" that had already killed "hundreds of thousands of Vietnam civilians". It was this idea of McNamara's that America's engagement in Vietnam had become genocidal and that genocide was un-American that was beginning to turn the country. On March tenth a Gallop Poll showed that 48 percent of Americans thought the US had made a mistake sending troops to Vietnam. Four days later President Johnson won an astonishingly narrow victory over Senator Eugene McCarthy in the New Hampshire primary. Two days later Robert Kennedy announced that he also was standing as a peace candidate for the Democratic nomination for President. On the eve of April Fools' Day President Johnson announced he was halting the "Goddamned bombing campaign" and was dropping out of the presidential race.

So it was the evening following the President's announcement that Julie and I were eating dinner at that window table in The Med. We were having a Monday night out. Charmaine worked most nights as a waitress but tonight she was at home looking after the two girls. Julie and I had been together two weeks now and so far most of our conversations had taken place in bed. We had almost finished eating our dinner and The Med was filling up and getting a bit loud and we had been talking about Julie-two when I became aware that Julie-one was maybe reading my mind. Already she had become adept at reading my mind and it amused her that she could do so.

"Are you going to ask me?"

"Ask you what?"

"Ask me that question that you were thinking of asking me just now when I mentioned my daughter's eyes – that question you've been thinking of asking nearly every night since you became my old man."

I looked around.

"Don't worry, My Love. If you don't shout no one is going to hear it?

I also was amused now, maybe even more than Julie. I leaned across the table.

"Who is Julie-two's father?"

"That's another of my secrets, My Love."

"Why?"

"Because he's very famous and I don't want my daughter to grow up and be saddled with that all her life."

"You mean she doesn't know and you're not going to tell her?"

"How would you like to have grown up as the son of Marilyn Monroe and be primarily known as this? You'd hate it. And I would never have found myself interested in you in a million years because you'd be so different from how you are."

"What about her father?"

"What about him?"

"Does he know?"

"No he doesn't, nor is he ever going to know. Contrary to what you're thinking, nothing is owed to him. The only thing he's ever done for Julie-two is ejaculate, and he did that prematurely. I only knew him briefly and only because I had been hired to photograph him.

"What do you tell your Julie?"

"She hasn't asked yet."

"She will."

"Of course and probably soon. I'm working on an answer."

I decided not to follow that up yet.

"You still love me?" she asked.

"Of course."

"In that case I think Julie-two should start to see more of you now. We could begin by you having dinner with us two nights a week and gradually increase it."

"I'd like that a lot."

"Wednesday night then. Charmaine is working, so there'll be just the four of us. A new experience for Michael I expect."

Indeed it was. After peeling potatoes and chopping an onion I was elevated to the rank of scary monster in a game of hide-and-go-seek. The big apartment was well-suited to the game. There were two ways in and out of what was now Julie's and my bedroom. One door connected with the apartment's inner hallway and the other directly with its living room. So when the scary monster making scary noises came looking for the four-year-olds they could run in circles through the apartment. But sometimes the monster would backtrack and hide behind one of the big arm chairs in the living room and leap out when the girls, trying not to giggle, came creeping through. At that point Julie would emerge from the kitchen telling everyone to calm down.

****

164

The first of the big events of '68 happened the next day at the Lorraine Motel in Memphis Tennessee at 6:01 p.m. local time. Standing on his room's second-floor balcony, Martin Luther King was struck by a single bullet entering through his right cheek, breaking his jaw and several vertebrae and severing his jugular vein and major arteries before coming to rest in his right shoulder. He was pronounced dead an hour later. Four hours later I heard the news in my old banger while driving to Julie's. She too had heard the news and was in tears when I entered. She was listening to Bobbie Kennedy. He was standing on a flatbed truck in a black neighborhood in Indianapolis, addressing a crowd.

> *I'm only going to talk to you just for a minute or so this evening, because I have some – some very sad news for all of you – Could you lower those signs, please? – I have some very sad news for all of you, and, I think, sad news for all of our fellow citizens, and people who love peace all over the world; and that is that Martin Luther King was shot and was killed tonight in Memphis, Tennessee.*
>
> *Martin Luther King dedicated his life to love and to justice between fellow human beings. He died in the cause of that effort. In this difficult day, in this difficult time for the United States, it's perhaps well to ask what kind of a nation we are and what direction we want to move in.*

Charmaine was at work and the girls were in bed. Julie was upset but I sensed she was feeling something else apart from just grief. The tightness of her grip on my hand suggested she was also fearful.

> *For those of you who are black and are tempted to fill with — be filled with hatred and mistrust of the injustice of such an act, against all white people, I would only say that I can also feel in my own heart the same kind of feeling. I had a member of my family killed, but he was killed by a white man.*
>
> *But we have to make an effort in the United States. We have to make an effort to understand, to get beyond, or go beyond these rather difficult times.*
>
> *My favorite poem, my — my favorite poet was Aeschylus. And he once wrote:*
>
> *Even in our sleep, pain which cannot forget falls drop by drop upon the heart, until, in our own despair, against our will, comes wisdom through the awful grace of God.*

Julie's grip had grown even tighter after Bobbie alluded to the killing of his brother.

> *We can do well in this country. We will have difficult times. We've had difficult times in the past, but we -- and we will have difficult times in the future. It is not the end of violence; it is not the end of lawlessness; and it's not the end of disorder.*
>
> *But the vast majority of white people and the vast majority of black people in this country want to live together, want to improve the quality of our life,*

and want justice for all human beings that abide in our land.

And let's dedicate ourselves to what the Greeks wrote so many years ago: to tame the savageness of man and make gentle the life of this world. Let us dedicate ourselves to that, and say a prayer for our country and for our people.

Thank you very much.

****

Julie smoked Pall Malls, a pack a day. But she didn't smoke dope or drink alcohol or, ignoring the nicotine, indulge any drugs other than caffeine. It was of course because of her father that she abstained. But the night of King's assassination I persuaded her to indulge in a glass of my recently acquired first bottle of port. I thought a glass might help her get to sleep. And it did or at least it seemed to because she fell asleep with me lying wide awake beside her in the green light. As I looked at her I learned something unknown and maybe unique and a little bit mysterious about Julie Newport.

Her face was already for me the most beautiful sight in the world. But although she was not homely – or "plain" as the English say – she also was not pretty and far from beautiful. My ideal of a beautiful woman has long been Ingrid Bergman, especially in her role alongside Humphrey Bogart in *Casablanca*. But when Ingrid's most beautiful face was viewed from certain oblique angles it could suddenly become rather homely. Undoubtedly this was known to her and to her directors, and those angles would

167

have been avoided when filming. But sometimes for a second or for three or four they would come into view on the big screen and when they did it was always a shock to me.

Julie was lying on her back asleep, her face facing the ceiling and for me profiled against the green light radiating from the shaded lamp on her bedside table. Lying on my side, with my head on my pillow I was looking at Julie's face in ninety degree profile. For some reason I moved my head off my pillow and closer to Julie's. Now my viewing angle was ever so slightly more than ninety degrees and now what I saw in the green light was a beautiful woman, beautiful not because of her soul – because from this oblique angle I couldn't see her soul – but rather beautiful like Ingrid Bergman was beautiful on the big screen. If I pushed my nose down all the way against the sheet the big-screen-beautiful Julie disappeared. It was only when in that green light I positioned and restricted my viewpoint within a tiny range that the physically beautiful Julie materialized. It intrigued me that I could make this physical reality come into being and vanish from being, whereas the beauty of Julie's soul was there beside me incorruptible and indestructible short of her death.

****

Calhoun was philosophical about Martin Luther King's assassination. We were sitting on the terrace at The Forum. It had been a week since the shooting. There had been riots in more than a hundred cities. Thirty-seven people, mostly blacks, had been killed. By now the riots had mostly stopped. But for blacks and for whites who were not racists and who dreamed of other whites becoming not racists the spring air was still scented with grief and foreboding, especially here on the Avenue.

I was on my second espresso. Our talking about King's assassination led us onto President Kennedy's.

"Speaking of Kennedy," I said, "why do you think people continue to believe the lone gunman with the magic bullet story?"

"Because there's no room in tiny minds for conspiracy theories. Anyway, it's too painful and too scary for most Americans to think otherwise," drawled Calhoun.

"Scary?"

""Yes, scary to think that it might have been carried out by the authorities."

"You think the full story will ever come out?"

"It seems unlikely because even good people who might know in part how it was organized may be afraid of what would happen to the country if the truth were known. But on the other hand the fact that they got away with it makes more assassinations more likely."

"And hence King's you mean?"

"No, I don't mean that because we don't yet know enough about King's assassination. It might not be connected. And it probably wasn't. I was thinking of another assassination that seems increasingly likely and is connected with JFK's."

"You serious?"

"Absolutely."

"Who?"

"Bobbie Kennedy."

"That's crazy, Calhoun."

"Maybe, but that's what I think."

"Why?"

"It's complicated. It has to do with the way I see American history. I see two traditions and two dreams running through our history, and they're completely contradictory."

"Two?"

"Yes. On the one hand there's the dream of equality, good lives and fairness for all. It's the American dream that gets written about and that we are taught in school and that inspires the good-hearted people of the world. Of course it's not just America's dream, but it is most known by that name and in terms of the moral evolution of human civilization it is the highest point. But America has always had another dream, the bad dream, the dream of conquering, enslaving and even liquidating others. It was there from the beginning with the Pilgrims, whose good dream required the conquest of someone else's land and their removal and eventually the death of the vast majority. Then came mass slavery and the sixty million who died as a result, followed by their quasi-enslavement that continues to this day in both the North and the South. And then there was that long period when American capitalism became perverted – 'pervert capitalism' I call it – and exploited and degraded the many for the benefit of the few. These things could never have existed through the centuries in our land if there were not just the Good American Dream but also the Bad American Dream. The Bad American Dream never gets talked about, but it is as much a part of America as the

Good American Dream, and the history of our country is the battle between its two dreams."

"Left and Right, in other words."

"No, no, Michael! It isn't about Left and Right or Democrat and Republican. It's not about that at all. It's a much more fundamental divide than those. After all, Lincoln was a Republican and so was Eisenhower who upon taking office immediately ended the Korean War, later sent troops to Little Rock, taxed the ultra-rich at ninety per cent and, when leaving office, warned the people about the military-industrial complex and its threat to their freedom. But when JFK came into the White House the Bad Dreamers, who had survived twenty-eight consecutive years of Good Dream presidents, thought they'd finally be safe again because Kennedy himself came from the ultra-rich. And when, in his inaugural speech, Kennedy said "Ask not what your country can do for you, but what you can do for your country," they heard that as an appeal for deference and subservience and acceptance of the status quo, in other words for the values of their modernized feudalism. And who knows, maybe that's what Jack meant at the time."

"But," continued Calhoun, "that's not the way the youth of America, or at least a prominent part of them interpreted it. For them it was a call to idealism. For them "country" meant not a hierarchy of power but rather community and equal rights and opportunities. And when they began to answer that call and college students volunteered for the Peace Corps and came South to help with the Civil Rights Movement and idealism began to spread in all kinds of ways it was seen by Bad Dream Americans, especially the ultrarich, as the beginning of their ultimate nightmare, the triumph of the Good American Dream over the Bad American Dream. And when word leaked out that Kennedy was going to withdraw all troops and military advisors from Vietnam, well, I imagine that's when the decision was made to get rid of him."

"But why Bobbie Kennedy now?"

"Because unlike his brother, Bobbie is an idealist to the core and they can see that. Anybody can see that. And what's more he has a score to settle: the murder of his brother and if he became President he would have the power to settle it. So there's no way they're going to let JFK's kid brother become President. Nixon looks like getting the Republican nomination and they know he won't stand a chance against Bobbie. But if they wait till after Bobbie wins the nomination it might look too obvious, so I think once it looks like he for sure has McCarthy beat, they'll assassinate him. They're probably planning it already."

"You make it sound logical Calhoun but I can't believe it. Not really. You think Kennedy has had any of your thoughts?"

"Sure, he's had some of them, but Robert Kennedy is a brave man and believes that he owes it to his country and also to his brother to do what he's doing."

"Do you ever think about writing about your theory of Two American Dreams?"

"Not really. I'm not much of a writer. Anyway, if anyone ever did write about it and it attracted attention, you can be sure that they'd find an excuse to lock that person up. But someone *should* write about it. In public, Bad Dream

Americans always go disguised as Good Dream Americans. That and the taboo against talking about the Bad American Dream makes us Good Dream Americans naïve and thereby vulnerable. Naïveté is our greatest weakness. It means that the dream that Bad Dream Americans have of killing, not just capturing, the Good American Dream could someday, maybe in forty or fifty years, come true. We could end up with a wildly anti-American president, maybe even Hitler-like."

****

That night when I told Julie about my assassination conversation with Calhoun I was at first mystified by her reaction. We were sitting alone on the couch in the living room. When I told her some of what I've just told you, she immediately stood up and left the room without saying a word. It was only later when we were going to bed that I got her to open up.

"I'm afraid Michael."

"Afraid of what?"

"Afraid that King's assassination will give Mr Ultrarich and his agents ideas."

"You mean shoot you?"

"And maybe you too."

"Oh that's silly?"

"I know it is, but I can't help thinking about it. Have you seen Trenchcoat again?"

I didn't answer.

"You have then."

"Maybe. I'm not sure. I didn't want to say anything because I knew it would get you worried."

"I think he's living in the apartment building across the street."

"Christ. Are you sure?"

"Almost. As I told you, when you told me your story back in January at The Forum, I recalled seeing such a person. Once when I was picking up Julie-two at nursery school and once and maybe twice in the supermarket. Then I saw him several times more, twice without the trench coat. A week ago I saw him coming out of the apartment building. It makes sense and it's almost too big a coincidence to be otherwise."

"Was he alone?"

"Yes, but as you figured, there must be at least two of them, probably more."

"But this apartment doesn't have any windows facing the street."

"If it did the Julies would've left already."

Julie and I were sitting on the edge of the bed and I put my arms around her.

"My Love, why don't you give them the negatives, please?"

"I can't Michael. You know that. If I did I wouldn't be me anymore."

****

Soon after I started eating dinner at Julie's, Julie-two and I became not only playmates but also friends. One evening it occurred to me that we shared a common

174

interest. I got down on the living room floor and started drawing with her in her coloring book. The next evening I brought her a small sketch book, some crayons that an artist might use and some watercolors. The watercolors turned out to be premature, but when I drew in her sketchbook outlines of houses and cars and dogs and people's faces Julie-two contributed windows, wheels, legs, eyes, ears, mouths and noses. Sometimes we both contributed to drawing the same mouth or pair of eyes. It amused her and it amused me too that we were sharing in the same creation and sometimes our joint efforts were marginally amusing.

One Saturday afternoon early in May Julie went out on a photo assignment leaving me in charge of Julie-two. Feeling restless, I decided to risk taking her to a coffeehouse. When we were leaving the flat and she saw me grab her sketchbook and crayons, she told me to bring my sketchbook too. Thus armed, we headed for The Forum.

Telegraph that afternoon was sun-drenched and crowded with walkers. We had to wait to get a table out on the terrace. When one came free I positioned Julie-two with our drawing materials at the table and then went inside to the bar. When I came back with two glasses of fresh strawberry frappé Julie-two was drawing. At first I thought she was oblivious to her surroundings but then I realized that she was drawing the head of the middle-aged bald-headed man at the next table. When she saw that I recognized what she was drawing – and it wasn't easy – she was delighted. She flicked her eyes toward the bald-headed man, laughed and, looking at me, cupped a little hand over her mouth.

Julie-two's model, who had a handlebar moustache, was facing us. I picked up one of Julie-two's crayons and in my larger sketchbook and with Julie-two watching and with a caricature in mind drew the outlines of his head and face, but left off the moustache. I handed the crayon to Julie-two and she immediately added the moustache. I developed his nose a bit and then pointed first to a blue crayon and then to my eyes. Julie-two thought for a second, then stood up and stepped closer to our model, squealed, sat down again and colored the eyes blue.

By now we had both an emerging caricature of sorts and a few people watching, including a woman in a pink dress who I judged to be the wife of our model. Julie and I added a few more embellishments to the drawing and then, at my suggestion, Julie-two offered it to the woman.

"Thank you so much. It's beautiful. Is it free?"

"No," I interjected, "it'll cost you a dime."

"What a bargain!"

The subject of Julie-two's first work of art handed her a dime.

We had two more sales that afternoon, and every Saturday afternoon thereafter until the second week in June Julie-two, armed with drawing materials and in a state of controlled elation, dragged me off to The Forum.

****

By the end of May I had virtually completed my dissertation, had had my first paper accepted by a journal, had two more papers under consideration, another nearly completed and two more in my head waiting to be written. It sounds impressive. But it wasn't really because they all were just formal math exercises, like workouts in the gym rather than performances on the playing field. Meanwhile there had been "the night of the barricades" in Paris and three general strikes in France, the last including nine million workers, and, closer to us, a series of state Presidential primaries in which the two peace candidates, Kennedy and McCarthy, took nearly all the Democratic votes, even in Nebraska. The decider was going to be California and if McCarthy lost, then, according to *Time,* Robert Kennedy would be the next President of the United States.

****

It was past midnight and Charmaine and the two girls were in bed. Julie and I were in high spirits. We were sitting on the floor in front of the black and white television. Kennedy had won. 46 percent to 42. We watched and listened as Kennedy addressed his supporters in a hotel ballroom in Los Angeles. It was as he left the ballroom through a service area to greet kitchen workers that *Time*'s next President of the United States was assassinated and the TV camera moved into the kitchen. Immediately I realized that my and Julie's future had been transformed.

****

177

The next morning I saw Calhoun at Enzo's and I had never seen him so depressed.

"Good dreams will die now," he said clutching his plaid hat in both hands.

"Maybe not."

"They will. The Peace Movement will die a slow death now. The thrill-seekers and self-aggrandizers like Ruben will take over from the Savios and the Weinbergs and instead of demos there will be riots and maybe even the odd bomb. People like you and me will disappear into the woods."

"Not you, surely."

"You forget that I escaped to California."

****

The second evening after Bobbie's assassination Julie and I had finished a late dinner with the girls and Charmaine, and Julie had put Julie-two to bed. I was alone in the kitchen and nearly finished with the dishes when Julie came in and said, "Let's go for a drive." Immediately I knew and saw that she saw that I knew that it was going to be more than just a drive. Of course we had talked about the latest assassination and what it meant for the country, but not about what it meant for us.

We got into Julie's bug, she drove and we headed for the hills. The best thing about the Berkeley Hills is that when you get up to their top there is no Berkeley there. I looked around several times to see if we were being followed and by the time we got up on Grizzly Peak Road and inside the eucalyptus forest it would have been obvious if we had been. Up at the very top we came to a deserted lookout point and Julie pulled over. Without saying anything we got out. Except for the bird song and the crunch of gravel under our feet the world was silent up there. We sat down on a low wall facing San Francisco. The sun had already disappeared behind the city's hills.

"Julie-two and I are leaving Berkeley."

It was more or less what I was expecting, but I had not thought about what I would say and I found myself at a loss for words.

"You want to try to persuade us to stay?"

"I'm not sure I do, because knowing that you're not going to give Ultrarich the negatives, I'm not sure you should stay. How do you see the danger now?"

"Today when I got home from picking up the girls from nursery school the phone rang as I entered and I picked it up and a man's voice said, 'Am I speaking to Julie Newport?'"

"I said yes. He said, 'Please write down this number. It's very important.'"

"I didn't say anything. Then he said, 'Do you have a pen and paper there?'"

"I said yes and he said, 'Alright, write down the number 138'."

"He waited a moment and then said, 'Did you write it down?'"

"I said yes and he said, 'Please repeat it to me?'"

"'138', I said."

"And then he said, 'Okay, now here's why the number 138 is so important. It's the number of a post box in the Berkeley Post Office. If you hand over the envelope addressed to Box 138, Berkeley at the nearest open window to the wall of post boxes, they'll put it in Box 138. You now have exactly 24 hours to deposit all the Central Park negatives and any prints you may have in Post Box 138. If by tomorrow at 12:42 the negatives aren't in that post box you'll have made the biggest mistake of your life.'"

"'BUT THEY'RE IN NEW YORK!' I screamed. 'There's no way I can get them to you by tomorrow! And no way even to get them over the weekend.'"

"There was a long silence on the other end. I think he was talking to someone. Then he came back on."

"'Alright we'll give you until next Tuesday at five o'clock.' And he hung up.'"

"You think he meant it?" I asked.

"Meant what?"

""Well I guess that's the question."

"And we don't know for sure."

"Not absolutely for sure."

"But a good half for sure."

"Yes, especially after the latest Kennedy assassination."

"So what do *you* think we, or at least Julie-two and me should do?"

"Well, if you're not going to give them the negatives, then you should get the fuck out of here."

"Before five o'clock Tuesday?"

"Obviously. Do you have a plan?"

"Not yet, but I have a dream."

"A dream?"

"Yes, Love. It's like this. You and Julie-two and me will drive off into the middle of America and find some obscure but nice place to settle down. I will turn to photographing nature. Julie-two will start school, and you will finish your dissertation and pursue your painting. When you're ready, you can fly back here and take your orals."

"What will we live on?"

"As you know I have a small income from my parents estate and in time you will sell your paintings and under a new name I will sell my nature photos. I'm confident of that. And we will live simply, in the country if possible. I'm even going to give up smoking, and you will too I hope."

"That's quite a dream."

"Will you help make it come true?"

I must have been a little overcome because the next thing I heard myself say was, "What about a dog?"

"A dog?"

"I've always wanted a dog."

"We can have a dog, Michael."

"It doesn't have to be right away, but eventually. I spent my childhood dreaming of having a dog."

"When we get settled we'll have a dog. I'd like that too."

"Well, if we can have a dog you can count me in. On your dream I mean."

"Our dream."

"Yes, our dream."

"But first we must figure out how we are going to get out of Berkeley alive and without Ultrarich's agents following us."

We were still sitting all alone up there on top of the world. The sky above San Francisco's hills had turned violent pink. Below the hilltops the city was vanishing in darkness. Rectangles of light appeared and disappeared up and down the Bank of America tower as the night cleaners made their rounds. In the deepening gloom we discussed our escape possibilities. We devised a rough plan centered on our buying a good-sized, fairly new get-away car. Then it occurred to me that Calhoun might be better qualified for planning escapes than we were. Julie agreed. On the way home I called Calhoun's house from a pay phone and he answered. Rather than tell him what it was about, I just told him it was important and he agreed to meet me in the morning at nine at Enzo's.

****

Enzo was foaming my cappuccino when Calhoun appeared. We took our coffees out to the mostly empty terrace and sat down at a corner table. There was no time for niceties and Calhoun had intuitively grasped the gravity of my situation. First I had to tell him the story of Julie's Mr. Ultrarich, including the real reason Trenchcoat had followed me to Santa Cruz. I had only just begun when he interrupted me.

"Tell me all the details you've thought of, and tell them to me slowly so I can take it all in."

So I did and it must have taken me near half an hour. When I finished Calhoun leaned back in his chair, reached into a side pocket of his tweed jacket and for the first time ever I saw him strike a match and light his pipe.

"Basically," said Calhoun now eight or nine puffs later, "it seems a good plan. But I see several potential flaws."

"What?"

"The first thing to remember is that Ultrarich's private detectives are probably the very best that money can buy."

182

"So?"

"So they're very clever, Michael, as clever as you and me. Someone who should know, once told me that most of the top private detectives are former FBI agents, not just because of their training but more importantly because they still maintain contacts inside the FBI."

"So what are we supposed to do about that?"

"You must be mindful of their intelligence and of their possible resources, like maybe having Julie's phone tapped, and you must think about what they'll be thinking between now and five o'clock Tuesday.

"Like what for example?"

"Like what will they be thinking as they watch you and Julie do this and that. And to begin with, are they watching us now?"

"Could be, I suppose."

"But they're not."

"How do you know that?"

"Because by the tone of your voice on the phone last night, I guessed that you were in some kind of difficulty. So thinking of your previous experience I made sure that I wasn't followed this morning. And I got here early, except instead of coming in here I waited over there across the street in the campus behind those bushes and watched you arrive so as to see if you were being followed."

"And I wasn't?"

"No."

"You're amazing Calhoun."

"No, I'm just a veteran of the early days of the Civil Rights Movement. But this is different. And Ultrarich's agents won't be at all sure that Julie is really going to hand over the negatives or try to run away. They may think the odds are only fifty-fifty or even less. So you want to make them think that the odds are shifting in their favour rather than against them. So what would Julie be doing today if she were going to go to New York and be back by Tuesday afternoon?"

"Make plane reservations."

"Of course. She could do it over the phone, I suppose, but most people would go to a travel agent."

"So Ultrarich's agents will be hoping to see her go into a travel agent."

"Exactly."

"That's easy. I'll tell her to go in and hang out in one for ten minutes or so."

"Yes, but that's not good enough. In fact it would probably be a disaster."

"Why?"

"Because it'll be easy for them to check if she really bought tickets, and you can be sure they will. After they see her leave the agency, one of them can go in and say he is supposed to buy his wife or daughter a return ticket to New York but wants to make sure she's not already bought it. They're almost sure to tell him, and at that point the odds in their minds will no longer be fifty-fifty. They'll be ninety-ten or ten-ninety."

Calhoun and I spent over an hour planning our escape. I took notes on the back of an anti-war leaflet. When we agreed that we had a workable plan – one that Calhoun was to play a big part in – the southern gentleman's expression turned inward.

"What are you thinking?" I asked.

"Of Hemmingway, of something he wrote. He said the world kills those it can't break. He said, and I think these are his exact words, 'It kills the very good and the very gentle and the very brave impartially.' Julie is maybe all of those, so I fear for her. You must be very caring of her, Michael, and watch over her carefully, not just in the next few days but also in the months and maybe for years to come. I'd like to stay and talk more but I've got to go now. As usual there's trouble with one of the presses. So do your stuff and I'll see you this evening."

****

Later that morning I typed up three copies of the following escape plan.

<u>Friday</u>

1. Leaving Enzo's and Calhoun, Michael returns to Julie's and goes over these plans with her. He stays for one hour, after which

2. Julie goes to a travel agent on Shattuck Avenue and books a return ticket from San Francisco to New York, leaving early to mid-morning on Monday and on a flight returning to San Francisco not later than 3 PM Tuesday.

3. Leaving the travel agency, Julie goes to her bank and withdraws $2,000 to give to Calhoun to buy us a car and $1000 for us to live on.

4. When Julie leaves for the travel agency Michael goes to his flat and packs up his stuff in his steamer trunk and the cardboard boxes stashed behind the furnace. After we have left Berkeley, Calhoun and Simon will pick up my stuff and store it at Berkeley Way.

5. At lunchtime, given that Julie's phone may be tapped, Michael phones her and asks if she has bought her ticket and tells her that he is so very relieved that she has decided to turn over the negatives to "those motherfuckers".

6. After having dinner at Julie's, Michael will go to the salon so as to give Calhoun the $2,000 and a copy of this plan.

Saturday

7. After lunch Julie-two and Michael will go as usual to The Forum for their joint drawing session.

8. Calhoun will find and buy us a car in Michael's name and park it on a side street (Dana St.) just off Bancroft Way.

Sunday

9. Calhoun will borrow Alan's car and drive it to Julie's and into the underground parking area and park as close as possible to the elevator.

10. We will then load up Alan's car with everything that we are going to take with us.

11. Calhoun will drive Alan's loaded car to where he has parked our new car and transfer our stuff to its trunk.

Monday

12. Early in the morning Michael will drive Julie in his car to the San Francisco Airport. She will be wearing her white tight-fitting mini-dress, carrying an overnight case and have her hair pinned up. Michael will let her off at the first (Calhoun says there are three) entrance to the terminal. Michael will get out of the car and kiss and hug her goodbye.

13. When Julie enters the terminal she will walk fast toward its third entrance. On the way, says Calhoun, she will pass a ladies room. She will go into it and take out from her overnight case a long loose fitting bright blue dress (Charmaine's) and slip it over her mini and let her hair down and put on sunglasses. She will leave her case behind in the ladies room.

14. Julie will continue to the third entrance, outside of which Calhoun will be waiting for her in Alan's car.

15. Calhoun will drive Julie to our new car back in Berkeley.

16. Meanwhile Michael will drive back to Berkeley and Cedar Avenue, where he will pick up his briefcase.

17. In case Michael is being followed, he will walk to the main university library, enter the stacks, exit them by a service entrance (Calhoun says it's on the first level), and exit the library by a side entrance. Michael will then cross Sproul Plaza to the Student Union, go inside and take the elevator to the top and then descend by a back staircase to a sub-plaza level where he will exit onto Bancroft Way, turn right and take the first side street (Dana) to the left where our new car and Julie and Calhoun will be waiting.

18. We will say goodbye to Calhoun and drive away into our dream.

Part Five – On the Road

As America passed by we listened to the radio but with a rule of never listening to any news except local news. Freeways also were forbidden. As much as possible we found our way on back roads, rolling along with the windows down. Lodi, Victor, Lockford, Jackson, Pine Grove, Pioneer, Kirkwood, Woodfords, Fredericksburg – Goodbye California / Hello Nevada – Carson City, Dayton, Silver Springs, Fallon (spent our first night here), Frenchman, Austin, Eureka, *(Of course I don't remember the names of most of these towns but I'm looking them up in an old Rand McNally as I write.)* Lawe, Ely – Goodbye Nevada / Hello Utah – Hinckley, Delta, Lynndyl, Leamington, Levan, Wales, Fountain Green, Birdseye, Duchesne, Roosevelt (spent our second night here) Vernal, Jensen – Goodbye Utah / Hello Colorado – Dinosaur, Blue Mountain, Elk Springs, Maybell, Lay, Craig, Hayden, Rabbit Ears Pass, Hot Sulphur Springs, Granby, Grand Lake.

In Grand Lake, or rather up on a mountainside above it, we stopped for ten days. There was a log-sided hotel up there with little pseudo log cabins scattered among the pine trees. We slept in one of the cabins and ate in the hotel on a big screened-in porch. It was while we were staying up there that we decided where we might settle. I thought I was occasionally going to need a good research library. I knew there was one in Madison, Wisconsin, and I remembered Vanessa saying that some of the countryside near Madison was really lovely. It being a university town and still early in summer vacation time, we would be able to find an apartment to rent for a couple of months while we looked for a nice place to live in the country.

Grand Lake, Estes Park (we stocked up on green light bulbs here), Loveland, Kersey, Fort Morgan, Akron, Otis, Yuma, Laird – Goodbye Colorado / Hello Nebraska. There was not a cloud in the blue sky as we rolled into Cornhusker land. We were now on a perfectly flat road that at a distance followed the mud-clogged Republican River. Every few miles the river flashed momentarily into view. Every ten or twenty miles the road jogged and at Haigler the road crossed the river and then at Benkelman crossed back over. Beyond McCook the treeless landscape became as flat as the road and there was nothing on the horizon except once or twice an hour the water tower of the next town. In between, except for the insects splattering on our windshield, signs of habitation of any kind were non-existent. We began to suffer sensory deprivation. Back in Colorado we had OD'ed on country-and-western and had turned off the radio. The three of us were sitting in the front seat, Julie-two in the middle, when Julie had an idea. From the glove compartment she took out a tape, the Beatles' *Help*, shoved it into the tape deck and turned up the volume. The sixth or seventh cut was already our favourite and we all knew the words. Julie sang the first verse by herself and then Julie-two sang the chorus all the while looking at her mother. I sang the second verse and then Julie-two sang the chorus looking at me, making funny faces, trying not to laugh.

> It's only love and that is all
> Why should I feel the way I do?
> It's only love, and that is all
> But it's so hard loving you
> Yes it's so hard loving you, loving you

We all laughed. Julie played "It's Only Love" again and we and the Beatles sang the whole song together.

It was the following day that a new dimension of my relationship with the Julies began to emerge. We had spent the night in Red Cloud, the town Willa Cather grew up in and that inspired *O'Pioneers*. Our Red Cloud motel room had reeked of disinfectant and after a greasy-spoon breakfast we detoured south a few miles seeking detoxification. There on the border with Kansas was a stretch of tall-grass prairie that had been preserved in its pre-pioneer condition. Walking in the shoulder-high red grass it was easy to imagine that we were the first people who had ever been there. Julie-two couldn't see above the grass, so I carried her on my shoulders.

We felt better after our walk and we got back in our car and reconnected with Highway 136. All morning we rolled flatter than flat across Nebraska. We were headed for Shubert. That is the town nearest to where my great-grandparents homesteaded. When growing up I had spent parts of my summers in Shubert with one of their sons, my great-uncle Worth. He was dead now, buried nearby with all the others in Prairie View Cemetery.

It was early afternoon and the June sun was blindingly bright. At the end of eight miles of straight gravel road running between knee-high corn fields we came to a sign: Shubert – pop. 231. It was Sunday and no Shubertites were to be seen as we pulled over and stopped on Shubert's block-long, one-side-only commercial street. We got out of the car and stood there in the hot dazzle. From the other side of the ridiculously wide street we heard men shouting inside the Lazy Dog Saloon. We needed directions for getting to the Prairie View Cemetery and I was about to venture into the Lazy Dog when in the distance we heard a cheer go up from what sounded like a small crowd. Led by Julie-two we got back in the car and headed in the direction of the cheer.

Coming around a bend we came to a baseball diamond. Behind home plate and a wire backstop was a small bleacher with fifty or sixty people sitting in it. The game was between innings. Over near third base a man wearing bib overalls and a red baseball hat was coming down off a stepladder beneath a scoreboard. In one hand he held a large black zero. Above him the scoreboard read: Shubert 2, Stella 1.

By now the crowd and some of the players had noticed our California license plate and I could feel the eyes focusing in on me as I got of the car and approached the first baseman who had come over to a low fence for a closer look at the aliens.

"They're lookin for the cemetery," he shouted back to the second baseman and the shortstop when I asked him for help. The cemetery was not far and he gave me easy directions.

Ten minutes later after a mile on 647 Avenue and a mile and a quarter on 719 Road we were there. Of course no one else was there. But there were twenty-one small trees – Julie-two counted them – and maybe nearly a thousand grave stones, all neatly laid out in rows except for the earliest ones near the road, where the five children of my great grandparents who died in childhood were buried. I read out some names and dates.

> P. Ellen King 1861-1862
> Coryden King 1859-1869
> Lever King 1863-1869
> Emma King 1866-1869
> Mattie King 1874-1880

We moved into the shade of a tree and sat down in the grass. Julie-two, fascinated with the tombstones, wandered off.

"Do you think we should worry about rattlesnakes?" asked her mother.

"No, they killed off the rattlers with the Indians. There's only bull snakes now and for us humans they're harmless."

We were both gazing at the empty horizon when without any warning Julie said, "How would you feel about becoming Julie-two's legal father?"

"Her legal father?"

"There's no father listed on Julie's birth certificate. I've consulted with my lawyer back in New York and he says that if we both sign forms saying that you are her biological father, then we can have your name listed as her father on her birth certificate."

"Why do you want that?"

"It's sort of obvious, isn't it. I mean, if something happens to me, if I get run over by a bus, then even if you wanted to take care of Julie-two you wouldn't be allowed to. They'd take her into custody and God knows what would happen to her. An orphanage probably. I've pretty much lost contact with my sister and even if I hadn't she probably wouldn't take her in."

"It's a lot to ask."

"Of course it is, and now that we've escaped from Ultrarich I don't fear for my life anymore. But accidents and fatal illnesses still happen. It's just that I'd feel so much better if I knew that if I died that you could and maybe would take care of Julie until she was grown up."

I was in a state of quasi-shock now. I'd never even once thought of such a thing. And I suppose the fact that I hadn't shows my thoughtlessness. But at least I didn't say no. I just sat there speechless, batting at the fly that kept landing on my nose.

Two days later we arrived in Madison. Julie had dropped the birth certificate thing by saying that when we found a place to live she would ask her lawyer to send the forms in case I decided I wanted to sign. Meanwhile we found Madison surprisingly nice. Its huge campus boarded the end of a long lake with wooded shores. On our third Madison morning we moved into a large attic apartment overlooking the lake. Both the Student Union, which had a large tree-shaded terrace at the lake's edge, and the Library were only a five-minute walk. Julie found a nursery school for Julie-two to go to in the mornings. In the afternoons she came with one or both of us, and every morning and every evening we bought a local paper and searched the want-ads for a rural house to rent. Most afternoons we drove out into the country to look at one. After a few weeks we became dispirited because we didn't find a single house that we really liked and that we thought would be good for us.

Part of our trouble was that we wanted a house with a fireplace. Mid-summer passed and then it got to be mid-August and we were getting desperate. We were fixated on having a fireplace and none of the houses we looked at had one. It was Sunday morning and Julie-two and I were sitting at a table close to the lake on the Union terrace. Julie had gone off to State Street to buy the local Sunday paper. Julie-two and I were drawing a caricature of a young Oriental woman. As my eyes shifted from our drawing back to our subject I caught site of Julie running toward us between the tables.

"You won't believe this," she shouted, "look at this."

She had the newspaper folded open to the want ads.

"No, don't look; I'll read it to you.

Furnished house, 5 bedrooms, 4 bathrooms, 2 fireplaces, $450 per month, 9 month lease, references, Tel. Spring Green 4650.

Furnished cottage, 2 bedrooms, fireplace, $150 per month, 9 month lease, references, Tel. Spring Green 4650."

The Frank Lloyd Wright book that Vanessa had given me in London was one of the few books I had brought with me from Berkeley. Since leaving, both Julie and I had spent time with that book and from its pictures we had fallen in love with Wright's houses. From our first week in Madison we had been intending to visit Wright's own house, Taliesin, on his estate of the same name and on which were other Wright buildings. But it was forty miles from Madison and because most days we were making long drives into the countryside that ended disappointingly we had never got around to going to Taliesin. But we had checked it out on a map and knew that the nearest town was Spring Green. We also knew – because Vanessa back in London had told me about it – that, although Frank Lloyd Wright was dead, the small architectural school that he had started continued and each year migrated back and forth between Taliesin and Taliesin West in Arizona. And of course Wright loved fireplaces. So when Julie read out loud the two want ads the penny dropped immediately. She had scarcely finished reading when I took the newspaper from her and ran inside the Union and to the bank of pay phones in the front hallway.

An hour later we turned off US 14 onto a narrow windy back road over-arched with trees. Between their trunks we caught blue-green glimpses of the Wisconsin River. On both sides of the river the topography had changed. Vanessa, I now remembered, had told me how there had been a hole in the ice sheet that had leveled the American Midwest and this little section of southwestern Wisconsin had been spared. The flat of the river was on our right but on our left close to the road were steep wooded hills and we could see the same over on the far side of the river. Ten minutes down the windy road we came to the mouth of a valley that emptied into the larger river valley. There was a gap in the high river bluffs and a low-slung bridge crossed over. We continued straight on. In front of us jutting out from the crest of a wooded hill and reflected in a small lake below was the great house.

A week later we took occupancy of "the cottage". For all three of us it had been love at first sight. Even the approach to the cottage was like out of a dream. When you came to the turn for the bridge across the river, rather than going straight ahead toward the great house, you turned left away from the river and then just before the road started to climb up into the hills you turned into a back entrance to the estate. A quarter-mile up a bendy half-paved track you came around a sharp bend and there on the left the woods gave way to a short run of grass running uphill to a little dark wood and yellow stone cottage with a low but massive chimney. Immediately behind, rising far above the chimney and even above the tree-tops, was a windmill, Wright's first commission. It was made of wood and had a balcony at

the top and was called Romeo and Juliet[7]. It was so close
and so tall that if it ever fell over in a storm it could crush
the cottage.

---

[7] https://www.flickr.com/photos/lorenzemlicka/4964071570

Part Six – Howl

http://www.wampy.com/Photography/FL-Wright-Architecture/Taliesin/i-hn6HChn/A
http://www.wampy.com/Photography/FL-Wright-Architecture/Taliesin/i-rqv7dxV/A

It was September now. Julie called it an Indian summer because the days were warm and golden. In the mornings a warm wind blew in from the west and made the windows rattle and the big trees roar. In the afternoons Romeo and Juliet laid a long dark shadow across the bright green meadow in front of our cottage. Later when the sun dropped behind our hill, the tower's shadow disappeared and the meadow lost some of its greenness and we slipped into sweaters and closed all the windows and doors.

Our first week in the cottage a dump-truck loaded with firewood from our local sawmill dumped its load in front of the terrace running past our living room's four pairs of

French doors. From those doors we saw across the valley to the high hills on the far side and down to the bottom of the valley and its little stream glinting in the sunlight, edged here and there with trees. They were willows mostly and still belonged to summer, but up on the hilltops the trees were already beginning to turn.

Counting the French doors, our living room had windows on three sides. It was a long room with a sloping ceiling, the underside of a roof sharply-pitched to shed the snow. The ceiling had slender dark beams sloping down across the width of the room to the tops of the French doors and then beyond the doors sloping a little more outside over the terrace. We were told that when the long winter came icicles would form from the ends of those beams and grow longer and longer, some winters growing all the way to the terrace before the big thaw came in April or, if we were lucky, late March.

Our long cottage was half in the woods and half out. Our bedroom was at the end that was in the woods. Like our living room, it had windows on three sides and a glass door exactly opposite the glass door at the far end of the cottage. If you entered from the living room's door you came onto a low stone balcony overlooking the room, the long line of French doors to your left and the fireplace at the far end. The balcony, the terrace and the fireplace were made of soft-gold sandstone, rough-cut and quarried from the big hills across the way. The fireplace had a deep wide shelf for logs, a hearth reaching far out into the room, a broad high-rising chimney-face and an arch over the passageway leading up to the bath and the bedrooms and the glass door in our bedroom leading into the woods.

Passing under the stone arch, you could, instead of going up three steps to the bedrooms, turn left and descend along the back of the fireplace. At the bottom and to the right was the rest of the cottage: an eating area, the kitchen and off it a small conservatory. There was also a laundry room that became Julie's darkroom. We had been living in the cottage for only a few days when we moved the dining table and chairs out to the conservatory, turning the eating area into a play area for Julie-two.

On our fourth day in the cottage Julie-two began kindergarten. Her school was across the river in Spring Green and driving there over the long low river bridge and through a dark flat forest was a short pleasant journey. Julie and I took turns driving the little one there after breakfast and picking her up at noon. There was no highway running through Spring Green, so, like Shubert but four times as big, it was its own quiet little place. There was its primary school and a grocery store twice the size of our living room, a post office half the size, a couple of white wooden churches, a bar rather than a saloon and a summer-stock theatre now closed until June. Some days after delivering Julie-two I went into the little grocery store to buy milk and eggs and loin lamb chops. There was a butcher at the rear of the store and in the first week I discovered his marvelous lamb chops. But he always served me with unsmiling reluctance, I suppose because my wavy blond hair now reached well below my collar.

****

We lived in the cottage with neither telephone nor television. From none of our many doors and windows that looked down and across our valley could we see even a single building, except sometimes in the evening we could see high on a distant hill a faint yellow light. But from the balcony in our living room when you looked out the glass door you saw through the wind-shifting gaps in the big oaks and elms another house not far away. It was the bigger house that had been advertised at the same time as the cottage. We had been living in the cottage a week before we saw people moving into the other house. We were going to go over and introduce ourselves the next day but that evening as Julie and I sat in darkness in the living room in front of a roaring fire there was a knock at the door up on the balcony. Julie turned on a light and I went up to the door.

It was a grey-haired woman in her early fifties who identified herself as one of our new neighbors. Of course I invited her in. We turned on more lights, and our neighbor, to whom I had already taken a liking, sat down on the couch. We told her our names were Julie and Michael. "I'm Betty Boardman," she replied. I didn't pick up on the possible oddity of that way of introducing herself but Julie did.

"Have I maybe heard the name Betty Boardman before?" she asked.

"Well, if you follow the news, you probably have."

"Have you been in the news recently?"

"It's been over a year now since I've made the national news."

"My memory is really bad, Betty, can you help me out?"

"I'm a Quaker and I and six other Quakers sailed a yacht loaded with medical supplies from Hong Kong to North Vietnam."

Both Julie and I remembered hearing or reading about the "voyage of the Phoenix" back in the spring of '67, and how at the last moment President Johnson had decided not to have it torpedoed.[8]

Betty Boardman stayed an hour. We learned that she was the divorced mother of six – five of her children were away at school or had left home – and she had had over 300 speaking engagements since returning from her adventure and now wanted to step back out of view and write a book about it. So she had moved to Taliesin with her ten year old son and another mother with a teenage daughter. But Betty had already discovered that she was not as far out of view as she had hoped. Since returning from her voyage the FBI had been watching and following her day and night. She had thought that maybe when she retreated from her home in Madison to the country they would forget about her, but she had already spotted one of "my agents" sitting in a car outside our entrance gate to the estate.

"I didn't want you to worry about it when you spotted them. Except when I'm gone, they'll probably be lurking there all the time."

****

---

[8] https://www.youtube.com/watch?v=v5bkPoNUcsQ

Facing our cottage was a hill that, rather than being one of the hills that formed our valley, rose up alone inside the valley and was cone-shaped like a hill in a children's picture book. We called it Midway Hill because it was midway between where we entered Taliesin and the big house also called Taliesin on the other side of the estate. Sitting on our living room sofa and looking out the French doors, Midway Hill was in the middle of your view. To the left and to the right of Midway stretched the line of the bigger hills that formed the other side of the valley and beyond which flowed the big river. All that country, even the big hills overlooking the river, was open to us for walking.

Each night when we were ready to go to sleep, I opened wide the window next to our bed. Some nights now I was having trouble sleeping. I think it was because I knew Julie had sent off for the birth certificate papers and I was wondering what I would do when the papers arrived. So some nights I found myself lying there awake in the green light, the scent of the woods drifting in through the open window and Julie snuggled up next to me fast asleep. And some nights I heard an owl. I loved hearing that owl and we had now been in the cottage for about ten days and it was about one in the morning and I was lying there wide awake hoping the owl would hoot when a wolf started to howl. *Of course I knew that was crazy.* There hadn't been any wolves in southern Wisconsin for most of a century, but now either there was a wolf or a virtuoso wolf imitator up on the top of Midway Hill. I was sitting straight up in bed and the howling, which came one long howl after another, was as real as the green light, as real even as Julie there fast asleep beside me, and I was sure the howling was coming from the top of Midway.

After a few minutes the howling stopped, but my consciousness was now so revved-up that going to sleep was unimaginable. So I got out of bed and slipped into my robe and tiptoed out of the bedroom, down the hall and into the living room. I pulled back some drapes on the terrace doors and moonlight streamed in. I saw my bottle of port there on the coffee table. I poured myself a tiny glass and sat down on a footstool on the hearth. The coals from our evening fire still glowed orange and I picked up a poker and stirred them. Yellow and blue flames appeared. I scooted the stool closer to the fire and leaned forward. I sat there feeling the warmth on my face and sipping my port. Port had never tasted so good. I took it in tiny sips and rolled it around on my tongue before swallowing. "Was it really a wolf?" I kept asking myself. I couldn't wait to tell Julie about it in the morning.

The port and the flaming coals calmed me down. I was about to go back to bed when I heard the howling again. I jumped up, opened a door and stepped out onto the terrace. But already the howling had stopped. The moon, full and yellow, hung low above Midway and the whole valley was dimly lit. I could see all the way to the far side of the valley, but my thoughts were up on Midway there in front of me. The night was windless. Not even a breeze stirred, and all I could hear was a vast mysterious silence. Then it started again.

"Hoooooooooooooooooooooooooooooooooooooooo ooooooowwwwwwwwwwwwwwwwwwwwwwllllllllllllllllllllllllllllll llllllllllllllllllllllllllllllllllllllllllllll"

It was still up on Midway. There on the terrace its mournful cry was so loud it sounded amplified.

****

"When you were out on the terrace, for how long did it howl?" The two Julies and I were eating breakfast in the conservatory.

"Three or four minutes maybe. But it seemed much longer."

"Do you really think it was a wolf?"

"Yes, it was the Big Bad Wolf," said little Julie.

"Yes, she's right; what else could it be but a wolf?" said I.

"Well, it could be the Big *Good* Wolf or it could be a lost Siberian Husky," said her mother.

"A husky?"

"What's a husky, Mama?"

"It's a kind of dog, Precious. Some people near where we lived in Connecticut, Michael, had huskies, and sometimes they howled and they sounded just like wolves do in the movies. They told me that Siberian Huskies are much closer to wolves than any other breed, and sometimes breeders still interbreed them.

"But there's another possibility. A wolf could have escaped from the zoo in Madison."

Yes, yes! It's the Big Good Wolf! The Big Good Wolf!"

"Maybe, My Precious, but that's over forty miles away."

"I know, but from what I've read, wolves can handle forty miles easily."

"Then why don't you call up the zoo. It's your turn to drive Julie to school. After you drop her off you can phone from the pay phone outside the bar."

****

So I did. The first zoo employee I talked to was incredulous at my inquiry but passed me on to someone more senior. When I eventually succeeded in convincing him that he wasn't speaking to a total crank, he assured me that none of the zoo's wolves had gone missing.

Back at the cottage the husky theory now prevailed, and for Julie-two the mystery howler became the "Big Good Husky". Her mother and I promised that if either of us in the night heard howling we would wake the other. Three nights later I was awakened by Julie shaking me by the shoulders.

"Wake up! It's back! Listen. Listen. It's so beautiful. Get up. I'm going out to the terrace."

I followed her out. Again the night was clear, cold and still, the moon nearly full and the howling coming from the top of Midway Hill. We had on only our robes, but I stood behind Julie with my arms around her and with her hands on mine. The magic of the howling kept us warm. Even in the intervals between howls we said nothing. It was only when more than a minute of silence had passed that Julie spoke.

"You must go to it, Michael."

"Go to it! What do you mean go to it?"

"It's a dog, Michael, that's lost its people or maybe another dog. And you want us to have a dog, and I want a dog and it would be good for our Julie to have a dog."

"But what the fuck you expect me to do up there?"

"Just be yourself, Michael. You've told me how you befriended dogs wherever you roamed as a boy. Do now whatever it was you did as a boy. The dog is probably spending the night up there on Midway. Even if it doesn't show itself it will catch your scent and it will watch you return here and maybe someday in the daylight it will pay us a visit."

"Will you come with me?"

"I'd love to, but if Julie had a bad dream and woke up and neither of us were here she'd be terrified."

I dressed quickly and started off. There had been no more howling. Once before I had climbed to the top of Midway. The meadow in front of our cottage descended for a hundred yards before it started to climb Midway's slope. This side of the hill was treeless and in the moonlight it was easy climbing through the long dew-wet grass. But I felt I was about to make a fool of myself. I remembered what I did as a boy, especially as a small boy, when I met up with a dog that I wanted to befriend. Could I really do that now at my age. "Oh fuck it," I thought. "This may be an absurd thing to do but it hurts no one and no one will hear me and no one will ever know and who knows it may work."

Near the summit the climb became steep and there were stone outcrops. I scooted around the outcrops, sometimes on my butt and then I was on the hilltop, flat, the size of a tennis court, dimly lit, a mix of the long meadow grass and low sumac bushes. As best I could I looked around. No wolves of course, no dogs, nothing moving. I felt so foolish. I decided to get it over with. I spoke very slowly as you would to someone who did not know your language well.

"Hello. I know you're up here. I've come because I want to make friends with you. My name is Michael Hope. I live in that little house down there with two Julies. One Julie is only five and has just begun kindergarten. We've just moved out here. Maybe you also have just moved out here. We'd very much like to have a dog living with us. I've never had a dog. But ever since I was a little boy I've dreamed of having one. Maybe we're not your kind of people, but we're pretty nice really. And it would be nice if you paid us a visit sometime and we could get acquainted a bit. I know you're not going to come out now and show yourself. And I don't blame you for that. If you have a good heart you have to be careful. That's what my friend Calhoun told me and I think he's right. But I think we have good hearts and there's nearly always someone down there in our house. So I hope you'll pop in someday soon. That's all for now. So long till later, I hope."

****

Each time we drove in or out of the estate we had to stop and open and close a gate. Opposite the gate was a little-used gravel road that ended at the blacktop road that looped around the edge of the estate. If Betty Boardman had not told us about her FBI agents we might not have noticed so soon that a car with a man in it was nearly always parked facing our entrance near the end of the gravel road. The day following my absurd nocturnal visit to the top of Midway I had to go into Madison. I left as soon as we finished lunch. I had seen Betty leave earlier, so when I got down to the gate there was no car parked over on the gravel road. In Madison I bought art supplies, did some research in the library and then a big grocery shop. So it was dark when I got back to Taliesin. As I closed the gate I made out the shape of a car parked in the usual place.

Up the hill we parked our car a short distance down from the cottage. A path, uneven with roots and stones, led uphill through the edge of the woods. Carrying two grocery bags I struggled with my footing until I got closer and the light from the conservatory spilled out into the woods. Inside I saw the table set for dinner and with the candles already lit. As I neared the lower door a dog barked. Just one bark, but loud and deep. It came from the terrace above me and to my right. Julie opened the door.

"Did you hear my boyfriend George out there?"

"Is it the howler?"

"Yes."

I started for the stairs up to the living room, but Julie, anticipating I would do that, blocked my way.

"Eat dinner first. Please, Michael. I've been holding it for half an hour and it's nearly Julie's bedtime."

"But it might leave. And how do you know his name is George?"

"He won't leave because he's been around all afternoon and he especially wants to meet you, and I know his name is George 'cause I made it up just now as you came through the door."

"How do you know he wants to meet me?"

"Because after I invited him in and we got acquainted a little – as you'll see he's very loud but very gentle and sweet with Julie here . . . ."

"He kisses wet," said Julie-two.

"When he finished kissing Julie he started running all over the cottage sniffing everywhere. Then he started making yodeling noises and I found him in our bedroom with his nose in one of your desert boots. He must've picked up your scent last night and remembered it. And by now he's picked up the scent you left just now when you came in. So he's not going to be going away until he meets you."

I'm usually a slow eater and the last to finish, but that night I ate very fast. I skipped dessert and rushed upstairs and opened a terrace door. In stepped a wolf-sized black dog with a shiny deep coat, pointed ears, an orange face-mask and the flashy, strutting self-confidence of a showbiz celeb. I crouched. George – he was forever to be George – immediately sat. At close range we looked each other over, then I pressed my fingers against his cold nose and stroked his head. He stood up, stepped forward and pressed his shoulder hard against mine. We were now friends.

The Julies had followed me up. George appeared to be a cross with a Siberian Husky and something else, probably a German Shepard, and he had now begun to perform. Or that's what I thought it was in the beginning. He made loud long-winded singing noises, not howls or barks, but more like operatic laments that went up and down the scale, all the while walking round in tight circles that ended with him throwing himself on his back and snapping at his belly. He performed this routine several times and the longer it continued the more demented my new friend seemed to be. But the fourth time, as he rolled over and snapped repeatedly at his belly and flanks, Julie and I got the message.

"It's those burrs. He's covered with them. He's asking us to remove them," I said.

And that was it. George became completely calm when he saw that our brains had finally understood what he had been asking us to do. For the next hour, except when someone pulled too hard, he lay perfectly still with his legs straight up in the air or on his side or however we wanted him to be. At least a hundred burrs were embedded in his fur and some very deep in his white undercoat and some we had to cut out with scissors. All three of us – Julie-two's little fingers were the gentlest – worked at deburring George. When we finished he subjected all three of us to an unreasonable number of kisses.

Before we went to bed we put George out for the night. When we rose in the morning he was lying on the terrace gazing out at the valley. I drove little Julie to school and afterwards went to the grocery store and bought cans of dogfood. Back at the cottage George was still there. Julie put some dogfood in a bowl and offered it to him. George sniffed it and walked away in polite disgust. But that night when we offered him the option of spending the night with us in the cottage he graciously accepted.

After that, except when there was a full moon, George slept with us in the cottage, some nights in our bedroom, some nights in Julie-two's. In the morning he went off hunting or at least that's what we presumed he was doing and sometimes he brought back a rabbit to eat in the meadow in front of the terrace. In the afternoon George usually hung around with me and the Julies. He was protective and watchful of Julie-two and indulged her need for play. This made it easier for Julie to get on with her photography and me with my painting and finishing my dissertation.

The nights came earlier and earlier. Sharp frosts came after sunny afternoons and turned the green of the valley yellow, yellow green, scarlet, orange red, yellow orange, red purple, brown, golden brown, purple brown and colors my eyes had never seen before. Julie had always shot mostly in black and white, but not now. On mornings it was my turn to take little Julie to school, big Julie often went off at first light to shoot. Some mornings she climbed up to the top of Romeo and Juliet to shoot the whole valley. Standing up there on the balcony you could see blue-green stretches of the river beyond the far hills and off sharply to the right the parked car belonging to Betty Boardman's agents. Twice I climbed up to the balcony to paint, but lugging a canvas and a pallet up the 54 ladder rungs inside the tower was rather much for me. I preferred to paint standing halfway down the far side of Midway. From there the big hills along the river were close, and just below me was the lake. To my left rose the long hill on whose brow Wright had built his house Taliesin. Its golden sandstone stretched low across the sharp edge of the brow and a cantilevered balcony leaped far out over the tops of red and yellow maples. The house and the maples were reflected in the lake below and it was that, the reflections, that I especially like to paint.

****

Our cottage came with one of those roadside mailboxes with a little red flag. Our flag was rarely up as almost no one knew where we were living. I corresponded only with my mother, my PhD advisor and the office of Berkeley's economics department, and as far as I know Julie exchanged letters only with her lawyer in New York. In early October I was returning one morning from taking Julie-two to school and, opening our gate and looking over at the FBI agent sitting in his black Ford, I noticed our red flag was up. Inside was a legal-size envelope addressed to Julie.

Later that morning I was working at the table in the living room that I had adopted as my desk when I felt Julie standing behind me. I turned around. She was holding a set of papers and looked worried.

"Here they are, my Love. The papers for Julie's birth certificate. I don't expect you to sign them but if by chance you decide to I'm leaving them with you."

She laid the papers on the table and started to walk away.

"Come back. Just show me where to sign and I will."

"Already?"

"Yes."

"Don't you even want to read them?"
"I trust you."
"You have to sign in two places."
"Show me."
She did and I signed.

****

We took turns tucking Julie-two into bed and reading her a bedtime story. Afterwards we spent the evenings by the fire, usually with George stretched out on the hearth. Julie and I had taken to reading books about Frank Lloyd Wright. We had found in our living room a whole shelf of books about Wright and his architecture, including his autobiography. We enjoyed reading these books and looking at their photos, but it was not all happy reading, especially the story of Taliesin

In 1909 Wright left his first wife in favor of the feminist wife of one of his clients. To escape the scandal that followed they fled to Europe, first to Germany, later to Italy. When they judged it safe to return to America, rather than go back to their Chicago, they hid themselves away in the Wisconsin valley where Wright's mother's ancestors, the Joneses, had homesteaded and where Wright now built Taliesin. He and Mamah Borthwick, whom he called his "soulmate", lived "in sin" at Taliesin until Saturday August 15, 1914. On that day Wright was away on business in Chicago. At Taliesin people were dining when the cook poured gasoline under the dining room door and lit a match. As the diners fled from the room the cook was waiting for them with a hatchet. He killed Mamah, her two children and four other diners.

At the bottom of what was now our valley was a cemetery. It was much smaller than the cemetery we had visited in Shubert, but it had a dark-wood chapel and around the graves some lovely trees. Wright had buried his soulmate there and had marked her grave not by laying a stone but by planting a tree. When Wright died fifty years later he was buried close by.

On a late October afternoon Julie and I walked down to the cemetery. It was sunny and Wright's gravestone was shaded by Mamah's pine tree. Julie sat down and leaned back against that tree's massive trunk and I laid down on Wright's gravestone that was flat and flush with the sod. No one else was about. From our respective positions Julie and I exchanged endearments.

****

Sometimes in the morning after Julie-two had been driven to school, her mother and I, instead of working, went out for a long walk. Usually we set off with no destination in mind. But we tended to head down to the lake and then across to the big hills above the river. At one end of the lake there was a waterfall, higher and much wider than I was tall, and Julie and I liked to pass by the waterfall on our way to the big hills. Sometimes without following a trail we would make our way straight up through the woods to reach those hilltops, other times we would go up on an old logging trail. It was always a good moment when we reached the top and we could see between the crowns of the trees down to the big river and its long bullet-shaped islands far below.

You could walk for miles up at the top along that overgrown logging trail, and although occasionally you startled a deer, you never encountered another person. The woods were mixed hardwoods, oak mostly and nearly mature. But they were not the original woods. They had been pine, giant pine, and they had all been logged nearly a century ago. Some of the Frank Lloyd Wright books talked about how beautiful and majestic those original woods must have been. One morning George came with us on our walk up on the tops of those hills. When George came with us on our walks he mostly did his own thing. Sometimes we would not see him for half an hour and he never, except maybe for ten yards, condescended to walk along beside us. So that morning when George walked beside us for over a hundred yards like an everyday domestic dog, we couldn't help but notice. And then he noticed that we had noticed and he looked slightly embarrassed but kept walking along beside us.

The sides of the hills where we were walking were very steep and usually ended with a sheer cliff above the river. Further up the river near where the bridge crossed and our valley joined the river valley there were no hills along the river and sometimes Julie and I walked down through the flat woods to see the beavers and the dams the beavers had built on Lowery Creek just before it flowed into the river. But when we walked up on the tops of the big hills, although we could see the river below, we had no way of getting down to it. Near the point where for the first time ever George started walking beside us, a lateral distance opened between the ridge of the hill and the river below and there also the drop-off next to the trail became precipitous. We had walked along this stretch for several minutes when George veered obliquely off the trail toward the river and then stopped and turned around to catch our attention.

Five minutes later Julie and I were watching and listening to the river rush by at our feet. George had shown us a safe way down. But it was not the river that was now the main attraction. It was the giant pines, at least a hundred and bigger than we had ever seen. This flat area next to the river below the precipitous ridge had been missed by the early loggers. When Julie and I, standing on opposite sides of one of the pines, tried to reach around the trunk and join both our hands with the other's we couldn't do it.

****

To become the self of your dreams, or even as in my case a very rough approximation, rather than the self dreamed up for you by others, is in every age a precarious journey. If I had realized just how precarious it would be, I would have lacked the courage to even start. But up to now my journey had been extraordinarily lucky. True, often I had not been happy, sometimes sad and lonely, many times lost and disoriented, but I had never had to live without hope for long. And of course and as I've tried hard to show you, I had the enormously great good fortune to have been heavily gifted by the people I met along the way. And some of them had also led me into strong pleasures, none of which I regretted, least of all those felonies committed in smoky rooms and many others in the nude between the sheets and now of course there was my felonious signing of those legal papers.

****

It was late autumn now, the days short and the trees nearly bare. At the end of October I had finished typing up my dissertation and sent it off. Early in November Julie-two's new birth certificate arrived and we put it away in a safe place. A few mornings later I was standing behind my easel on our terrace when Julie, returning from taking our Julie to school, rushed up across the grass carrying a package resembling the one I had sent off to Berkeley with my dissertation.

"Oh my God, have they returned my dissertation?"

"No, it's maybe worse.   Here.   Look at the return address before you open it."

It was addressed to me.   The return address began Nelson Dunnefeller Jr., my fellow econ grad student.   The enclosed letter explained that he was hoping I could tidy up the math in this penultimate draft of his PhD dissertation. He said, and I related it to Julie, that he had obtained my address by asking for it in the administrative office of the Economics Department.

"Well if Nelson can go into that office and get our address so could Mr. Ultrarich's agents."

****

In mid-November Julie started a project of photographing in the morning light the river and the big hills from the top of Midway. So I started driving Julie-two to school every morning instead of every other. On Friday the 22nd as she and I were leaving for school, instead of the usual black Ford parked on the gravel road opposite our entrance gate there was a beige car, make unknown. It was parked a little closer than usual and it was not until later that day that I learned that Betty was away for a week on a speaking tour. The next day, the same day that the deer hunting season began, and all that weekend we did not leave the estate.

Monday morning as Julie-two and I were getting into our car I paused to watch her mother walking toward Midway. Her green leather bag was swinging from her shoulder, and I thought of that evening at the Berkeley salon when we had just met and we were still perfect strangers − except somehow we weren't − and she took hold of my hand and placed it on her green leather bag and I felt around for what was inside.

Minutes later down below as I was closing the gate, I saw Julie and George nearing the top of Midway. I also saw that the beige car was there again in the same place and that this time there were two men sitting in it. Remembering that Betty was away, "deer hunters" was my passing thought as I drove off. But as we were crossing the bridge I recalled that the same car had been there on Friday before the deer season had begun. Although I had not been able to see clearly the two men inside the car, it now struck me that there was something about the man in the passenger seat, his shape and the way he moved his head when he appeared to be speaking to the driver, which reminded me of someone. Who, I wondered momentarily before Julie-two asked me when we were going to do caricatures – she pronounced it "car-ters" – together again.

After dropping her off at school I went into the grocery store to buy lamb chops. A headline in the local paper caught my eye and I bought a copy.

Woman Killed by Guns
As Deer Season Opens

As Deer Season Opens BOTH HUMAN and animal blood was spilled Saturday morning as the Wisconsin deer hunting season opened. Judy Haroldson of Rosholt was the first reported gunshot victim. As the season was opening she was shot in the back while hunting with companions.

The article went on to say that the Wisconsin deer season death toll in 1967 had been 36 – six by gunshot and 20 as the result of heart attacks.

It was only when I was crossing back over the river that I realized that the person whom the man sitting on the passenger side of the beige car had subliminally reminded me of was Trenchcoat.

When I reached the gate the beige car was gone. "Take it easy Michael" I said to myself, "You're just being paranoid." But I didn't stop to close the gate and then as I was driving up the hill and getting close to our cottage I saw George running at full-speed from the direction of Midway toward my car. I slowed down but before I had stopped he was jumping up against the side of the car and making awful noises.

From there to the top of Midway was the furthest I had ever run. I immediately spotted George at the far end of the flat summit. He was hovering over a supine human shape and when he turned his head to look at me it was clear from his eyes that he had decided that our Julie was dead. She was very dead. She had been shot twice, once in the chest to the right of her heart and once in her right cheek. That shot had blown off the back of her head. Her mother's green leather bag was on the ground beside her, but her camera was missing. George and I both knelt crouched beside Julie, me sobbing, George howling.

Epilogue

Calhoun Phifer: He'll always be with us

Calhoun Phifer, PCC Greenlake staff

Known for his sense of humor, outgoing personality, his plaid cap and penchant for classical music, Calhoun Phifer was a loving, generous man and irreplaceable member of the PCC Greenlake team.

Calhoun, age 78, passed away on January 3 (2003) while visiting friends in California. A small service was held at Greenlake park on January 19. "He always had a twinkle in his eye and saw humor in everything," says staffer Suzannah Pratt. Cindi Fuda, Store Director adds, "He was the sweetest southern gentleman — helping me with recycling and fixing things around the store. I honestly don't know what I'm going to do without him."

Calhoun had a vivid life that included earning degrees in history and philosophy from Tulane University and working on the railroad. He was self sufficient and independent and a joy to be around. Calhoun will be sorely missed by all of us at PCC.

http://www.pccnaturalmarkets.com/sc/0302/coopwork.html#5

Alan ?????? – fate unknown

Betty Boardman
http://host.madison.com/news/local/obituaries/article_0aab87e9-958c-55e4-a415-98197d60bbdd.html

Michael Bowen
https://en.wikipedia.org/wiki/Michael_Bowen_(artist)

Nelson Dunnefeller, Jr. – fate unknown

John "Tito" Gerassi

http://www.lemonde.fr/disparitions/article/2012/08/1
0/john-tito-gerassi-l-ami-americain-de-sartre-mort-
a-81-ans_1744962_3382.html
http://www.counterpunch.org/2012/07/27/tito-
gerassi-1931-2012/

Sue Ruccio – fate unknown

Mario Savio – In 1997 Sproul Plaza Steps were officially
renamed Mario Savio Steps.
https://en.wikipedia.org/wiki/Mario_Savio
https://www.youtube.com/watch?v=tcx9BJRadfw

Simon ?????? – fate unknown

John Thompson
http://carmellife.com/john-thompson/

Trenchcoat – fate unknown

Ultrarich – uncertain

Vanessa ?????? – fate unknown

Jack Weinberg
https://en.wikipedia.org/wiki/Jack_Weinberg

Mrs Youngscap – fate unknown

****

"Did the CIA kill Bobby Kennedy?"

http://www.theguardian.com/world/2006/nov/20/usa
.features11

"New evidence challenges official picture of Kennedy shooting"

http://www.theguardian.com/science/2008/feb/22/k
ennedy.assassination

****

It's an hour past sunrise and I'm standing at my easel at a place we call The White Cottage. I'm told that both Julie-three and Julie-four were conceived here. I bought the cottage after my first one-man London show, way back when these modest houses along the south Devon coast were still relatively cheap. I'm upstairs in a bedroom looking over my easel and out a big window at a blue sky with three small white clouds and the green sea below. Once a year the three Julies and I come here for a few days alone. Julie-two's husband is coming down from London to join us tomorrow. An hour ago she went off to paint at Elander Cove. It's only a fifteen minute walk and she'll be back for lunch. Meanwhile Julie-three has gone off to pick up her partner at the Plymouth Airport. She's a nature photographer and works for the BBC. Recently she travelled to America and visited Taliesin and brought back photos of her grandmother's tree down in the little cemetery. She says the tree is now nearly fifty feet tall. Julie-four is nearly three feet tall. When I look down and to the right of my easel I can see her sitting on the swing that hangs from the chestnut tree. George the Fifth, a border collie, is a discreet distance away lying in the shade. I'm officially in charge of Julie-four today, but it's George who's doing most of the work.

As you know, I'm old now, my death coming near, but I wanted you to know that I dream now more than ever. Of course I dream for my three Julies, but I also dream that the Good American Dream is not dead. I dream that instead it has only been a long winter. I dream that soon everywhere the good and the brave youth of today's world will rise up and that unlike that of my generation your rising will be successful. I dream that the Ultrarichs will lose and that you will win.

22315060R10139

Printed in Poland
by Amazon Fulfillment
Poland Sp. z o.o., Wrocław